SOUNDS OF DECEPTION

by

Mike Downs

Books by Mike Downs

The Artimus Box
Novac's Race
Novac's Run
Bobo's Raid
Sounds of Deception

Author's Note

Please keep in mind that this is a work of fiction. the names, characters organizations, dates, and events in this novel are a product of the author's imagination, or are used fictitiously. Any resemblance to actual events or persons living or dead is purely coincidental.

This book is available in print and digital formats at most online retailers.

For K always

FOREWORD

August 14th 2015 marks the 70th anniversary of VJ day. VJ stands for victory over Japan. This is a day to celebrate the courage and sacrifice of the men and women of the armed forces and the workers on the home front. These people are known to many as America's greatest generation.

In the late 1930's war sweeps across Europe, and Asia, destroying lives and cultures like a plague. America does not want war; we are unprepared. Most hope the oceans between us will quench the scourge to keep us safe.

On December 7th 1941 the Pearl Harbor attack kicks awake the sleeping giant. The West Coast fears an imminent Japanese attack. America shakes off her fears to step up to her enemy's brutal onslaught. Fathers and mothers, our grandparents, or great grandparents become our finest generation. America is the last bastion of democracy, the last hope of world freedom. The government quickly puts its politics aside to place acts into play in order to defend the nation. The best asset America has to defend freedom is her people. Men and women who were once intolerant of other races and religions now must work together in an unparalleled effort to supply our war machine.

America becomes the mightiest industrial nation on earth. Planes, ships, arms, munitions, food, and supplies of all types are made in quantities no one could even have imagined months earlier. A liberty ship, the *Robert E. Peary*, is built in a record 7 days. B-17 bombers go out every four hours, B24 bombers every 100 minutes. America's manufacturing plants and workers are unstoppable.

In research for *SOUNDS OF DECEPTION*, which depicts the spy-ring-busting adventures of a WWII submarine sailor at Mare Island, I found many cases of supreme sacrifices by our brave military and men and women on the home front.

The novel will be released just before VJ day, August 14th 2015 and is dedicated to all those Americans with heart-felt gratitude.

1943 San Francisco CA

Nick Devin, tired of the noise and confusion of honky-tonk bars, left his fellow sailors and walked alone down Sutter Street. What he wanted was a good jazz band, a woman, and another drink. The woman was tall, the band was tight. She had long black hair and a honey-husky voice. She came over to sit beside him; he bought her a drink and she fondled his leg.

Nick knew this was dumb, but his little brain was in the lead. His liberty was up tomorrow, or was it today? He'd have to be back at Mare Island getting his new submarine ready for trials.

Waves of wet fog pushed through the Golden Gate on the cold San Francisco end-of-summer night. Fog horns in the distance mournfully croaked their warning. Nick hesitated as the woman led him to the mouth of an alleyway. Smiling brightly, the dark-haired vixen looked over her shoulder to beckon him on.

Nick opened his eyes expecting to awake from a dream. He flinched: his eyes opened wide, focusing on the man standing over him. A gaudy red and green mask covered the man's eyes.

"Ah, our valiant sailor awakes." The commanding, German-accented voice came from a man who had a thin face with a bushy mustache that bristled beneath the mask.

"Where am I?" Nick asked.

"You are among friends," the man answered. "You seem to have been off your game last night, my friend. Freda had us bring you here after you passed out."

Nick sat up, his mouth dry, head throbbing. "I guess I'll need to thank you for helping me out. I have to get back to my boat now; I don't want to be AWOL."

Two more men with the same red and green masks entered Nick's field of vision to stand by his cot.

The mustached man said, "We have a few matters to discuss before I can allow you to leave."

Nick stood slowly from the cot. The two men started as Nick reached for his wallet. Mr. Mustache held his hand up to stop his men.

Nick pulled cash from his wallet and held it out. "This is all I've got. Your woman was good; I never saw her put a damned thing in my drink."

"Put your money away. What I want, and what you will tell me, is everything you know about the sonar and radar capabilities of your submarine. If you think I am not serious, I will have your friend Doris and her boy mutilated in ways you will not want to imagine. Yes, that's right, I know all about them."

Nick dropped his wallet; his right fist flashed to the mustache-man's jaw. He felt the satisfaction of his fist connecting before his brain went black.

***

"Come on, sailor. Get up off the ground."

Nick opens his eyes as a policeman prods him with a nightstick.

"Where's your ID and your Liberty Pass, sailor? Where are you stationed?"

Nick gets up off the ground with a groan, feeling for his wallet. "Those bastards got my wallet and papers! What time is it, officer?"

"Who got your wallet?" the officer asks. "Are you saying you got rolled? You oughta be more careful, son. This town can eat you alive. It's 6:15 a.m. and I have to take you to the Shore Patrol."

"Oh, man, I'm too late for roll call."

The cop watches the sailor wrestle with his predicament. Nick gathers himself, his brow unfurls, his decision made. He picks his hat off the ground and squares it on his head. With a determined set to his jaw, he focuses on the policeman.

"Look, Officer, I've got to get to the FBI."

The policeman rests his hands on his hips. "Are you gonna try to make a federal case outta this? Take my advice and 'fess up to the Shore Patrol. Take your medicine like a man. You ain't the only sailor too drunk to get back to his base on time."

"I'll do anything you want me to do, Officer, if you'll let me talk to an FBI agent first. This is no joke and I wasn't drunk. This has to do with spies that want me to get them secret Navy information. Is there an FBI office near here? If you take me to one, I'll tell them my story. If they don't believe me, you can do whatever you want with me."

"There's an office on Sutter. I don't know why I should believe you, but if you're lyin' you're gonna make things a lot worse for yourself. Come on, get in the car."

At the FBI office, the police officer paces the floor, raising his wrist, looking at his watch for the umpteenth time. Finally the FBI agent the policeman met when he brought Devin in comes into the room, shutting the door behind him. "You did the right thing bringing the sailor in, Tom. We'll take it from here."

"You believe him, Agent Keys?"

"Just call me Keys, Tom. He's got enough of a story that I have to check it out. I appreciate your help. You can leave him with us."

Tom hesitates. "Uh, can you guys just take over like that? Shouldn't I report this to the Shore Patrol?"

"Tom, this is wartime, my friend. We protect the nation. My big boss and FDR are like two peas in a pod. We can do just about anything we want. You have made your report to me; forget you ever saw the sailor."

Nick, sitting in the little FBI office, head in hands, wonders what he has fallen into. He muses back to happier times when he met Doris and Benny at Mare Island weeks earlier. "Now we're all in it," he mutters.

Chapter 2

Thirty odd miles to the northeast of San Francisco's Golden Gate, the bustling Mare Island Shipyard, now at the height of World War II, throbs with energy. Nick's new submarine, the *USS Bullshark*, is being fitted out prior to its first sea trials. This latest design in war machines is tied up dockside in front of the old coal bunkers facing the river.

Morning fog, just lifting, swirls with the wind as it sweeps across the waterfront. Heavy mists shroud the tops of the giant heavy-lifting cranes' skeletal framework. Their thick steel cables with giant hooks seem to drop unsupported from the heavens. The cranes groan metallically as they position huge ship sections; masses of leather-clad workers descend upon them almost instantly, welding the great steel shapes in place. Nick had transferred from his old boat weeks earlier, assigned to the schools on new weapons and to help ready his new boat for war patrols.

Early afternoon sun brings welcome warmth to the throngs of workers massed to watch Bob Hope and his troupe put on a war bonds show. Nick watches with a small boy on his shoulders and a pretty woman by his side. Doris Wimmerman and her eight-year-old son, Benny, found Nick soon after he arrived at the shipyard. Together they watch Bojangles dance and have a good laugh at the comedy skit put on by Joan Blondell and Una Merkel.

Doris works as a typist at the shipyard while her husband is away fighting in Europe. She bumped into Nick on the shipyard and, from time to time, brings him lunches so they can spend time with Benny at Alden Park.

After the show Doris, with Benny trailing, follows Nick back to the *Bullshark*. She touches Nick's arm to slow him down. "People at the office say you're a genius with all that sonar, radar stuff. Do you really understand it?"

Nick stops. He turns to Doris as Benny grabs his hand, smiling up at his face. "Jeez, how does that stuff get out? I do like electronics and have a good understanding of how things work. I really think electronics will be big in the future. After the war I have a job waiting at Jack Novac's lab in Culver City."

Benny, still holding Nick's hand, asks, "Will you be my Daddy?"

Nick's embarrassment causes his head to swivel. He looks around to see if any of his shipmates are within earshot. "Uh, you have a Daddy. I'm just here a little while before I have to leave."

Benny knuckles an eye. "Can't you be my Daddy 'til you go?"

"I can be your friend, Benny. Your real daddy will be home soon."

Nick takes his hand from Benny's to shake Doris' hand. "I've got to get back to my boat. The show was fun; I'm sorry I don't have time to walk you back to Benny's daycare."

"That's alright, Nick. I know you're busy. I'll bring another lunch soon and maybe we can talk about what life will be like after the war's over."

"That'll be okay, Doris, if I can get away. I can't promise anything." Nick walks away resisting the urge to look back.

***

Days after Nick's encounter with the spies in San Francisco, Lieutenant Commander John Shaver reports to his superior, Commander Albert Morsey, at the submarine operations office.

"So, Shaver, you're telling me this boy Devin is something special?"

Although Shaver's rank is Lieutenant Commander, his title while in command of his new boat, the USS *Bullshark*, is Captain.

"I believe he is, sir. I was the exec (XO) on the *Bayfish*. We were both on her for four war patrols. He qualified easily, was our go-to man for anything electrical and dedicated himself to keeping our radar working. I've never seen a sound man as sharp as Nick. All of our officers were glad to have him aboard. I don't believe he'd lie about being late, sir. When he told me about the German guys grabbing him, I believed him. He wants to help the FBI get the bad guys; he's that kind of man. I brought my report on him for you."

Morsey huffs out a breath. "I hope for your sake this isn't a huge waste of my time. I have too much on my plate now. This is not the first time a sailor made up some fantastic story as an excuse for returning late from liberty. I'll look through this report, after which I want to see this sailor for myself."

7

After Shaver leaves the office, the Commander summons his aide.

"Mitch, I want everything you can find on Chief Nicholas Devin. Here's his information and serial number. Get on it, I need it ASAP."

The next morning the aide places a thick file on the commander's desk along with a mug of coffee.

The commander takes his reading glasses from his pocket. "That was fast. Where did this come from?"

"Our Office of Naval Intelligence had it, sir. The background is from an FBI search. He has two years of electrical engineering from USC. When he was in our sonar school, the instructors were amazed by his knowledge. One of the instructors thought he knew too much. The ONI investigators asked the FBI to run his background. They in turn did an in-depth investigation of Devin and his family."

The Commander's phone rings and the aide rushes out of the office to answer it at his desk. After a short phone conversation the aide returns to stand at the front of the Commander's desk.

Commander Morsey looks up from the file. "What is it, Mitch?"

"It's Washington, sir, Admiral Lusk."

"Just what I need. Okay, Mitch, I'll take it. Close the door on your way out."

Morsey pulls off his glasses to fling them to the desk and picks up the phone.

"Hello, Admiral, what can I do for you?"

Speaking into the phone, Morsey grimaces.

"The president is concerned, sir? Yes, sir, I understand you. All that happened before I was in command here, sir. What is it you would like me to do, Admiral?"

"Yes, sir, I will contact the Pearl Harbor ComSubPac commander and report back to you as soon as possible."

After putting down the phone and not bothering to use the intercom, Morsey yells for his aide.

Mitch hustles through the door to stand in front of the captain's desk and salutes smartly.

"Get me the ComSubPac commander at Pearl."

"Yes, sir. Do I tell his aide what you want?"

"It's about that damned toilet paper letter Coe wrote.[1] Apparently the President's son sent him a copy of the letter and now the President wants to make sure Captain Coe is satisfied. I can't believe the life that letter has taken on. The next time Coe shows up here I'll fry his bacon. So, no, don't tell his aide anything, just get Pearl on the horn."

Mitch salutes and turns to leave.

"Mitch, take this file with you. You read it, I haven't got time. Give me a report in the morning. After I talk to Pearl I'm leaving. I'll be at the golf course until after dinner."

Mitch takes the file from the commander and turns around to leave. He rolls his eyes, then quips, "Aye aye, sir."

Morsey gives his aide a hard look as Mitch exits the office.

---

[1] Captain Coe's letter is included at the end of the novel.

Chapter 3

The next morning Mitch sits at his desk with his pea jacket on, hunched over a steaming cup of coffee. Nick Devin's file is propped up against thick Navy manuals. The commander's aide's eyes follow the words across the pages. Two hours later the commander enters barking for his coffee.

Mitch brings the commander his coffee in a white mug embossed with a commander's crest. Two teaspoons of sugar and two tablespoons of the commander's own real cream have been carefully stirred in just as the man demands. Morsey takes a tentative sip, then leans back in his chair with both hands curled around the mug.

"Did you get that sailor's file read, Mitch?"

"Yes, sir."

"Alright boy, what's it say?"

"I'll just get the file off my desk to get all the facts and read it for you sir."

"Get the file, but I want a report. I don't have time for you to read the whole thing."

Returning with the file Mitch sits in a chair across from the commander. Opening the file he begins:

"Nicholas Devin was born October 1922 in Fullerton, California. His father was a soldier in the Army and served in the First World War. He and

Devin's mother live in Palms, California. The father works for Douglas Aircraft as a machinist and the mother works at Warner Brothers Studios in the costume department.

"Devin was an A and B average student in grade and high school before going to USC. Racing cars seems to have been his hobby before he enlisted. He was an outstanding college student majoring in electrical engineering. He was also enrolled in NROTC.

"Apparently he decided to enlist before completing his classes. According to his father, and over his objections, Devin couldn't wait to get into the fight. He was first in his class in sub school and put in for sonar and radar training. His grasp of the electronics made one of his instructors very nervous."

"Tell me what the hell's nervous mean, Mitch? And keep it short okay? Is the guy stupid or some kinda egghead?"

"Egghead I'd have to say, sir. The captain of the *Bayfish* fought hard to keep him. He didn't want Devin cut loose to go to the *Bullshark*. Devin was the only sound man the captain trusted in the fire control party. Devin was known to do thirty-six hour stints during torpedo runs and depth charge attacks. His captain credits the man with getting them out from under the Japs depth charging by keeping the sub's stern to the depth charges. He could judge the distances of the exploding charges to keep the stern ahead of some of the attacks."

Morsey sets his coffee mug on the desk. "So what kind of trouble has this boy genius been into while on liberties?"

"There is nothing in this file to indicate any trouble, sir. As a matter of fact the officers he has served with all say Devin is officer material."

Morsey leans forward in his chair. "Officer material, huh? I don't like the thought of enlisted men becoming officers. The academy is the only place where officers should be made. It's a rare sailor that doesn't get into some kind of trouble on land. No, I just don't like the sound of this guy. Get the boy in here, Mitch; I want to take a look for myself."

"Sir, the FBI has Devin in an office downstairs. They called earlier to make an appointment with you."

"That's more like it. Why didn't you tell me that when I came in? I wouldn't have wasted my time with your report."

"Sorry sir, I thought you would like to know something about the man before a meeting with the FBI."

"I think if the FBI has him then we probably won't be troubled to work out the boy's fairytales. I suppose I'll have to find the *Bullshark* another sound man. Well, get to it Mitch. Let's have the FBI up here and get this over with, I've got too much work to do as it is."

Mitch ushers two FBI men, along with Nick Devin, into the commander's office and introduces the men.

"Sir, this is Agent Keys on your right and Agent Walsh; Chief Devin is reporting in. Gentlemen, Commander Albert Morsey, submarine yard commander of Mare Island.

Morsey, beckoning with his hand, greets the men. "Come in, come in, have a seat gentlemen."

The FBI men pull chairs in front of Morsey's desk and motion Devin to the center chair.

Devin salutes the commander, holding the salute until the commander acknowledges him. Morsey takes his time inspecting the sailor before him. The sailor he sees is a slim man, handsome in a rugged sense, sporting blond crew-cut hair. Devin has the air of confidence and the same swagger most submariners display. Morsey finally returns the salute and Nick starts to sit down in the chair the FBI men provided.

"Not you, sailor," Morsey barks. "Remain standing."

The FBI men exchange a look. "Excuse me Commander," Agent Keys exclaims. "Chief Devin has volunteered to help us round up a gang of spies. This is a potentially dangerous undertaking. We are grateful for his coming forward with this information and his willingness to help us weed out these traitors."

Morscy sits forward in his chair. "If you know who these people are, why the hell don't you arrest them? This sailor is needed on his submarine. I hope you've not forgotten we have Jap shipping to sink if we're to win this war."

The FBI man's face flushes. "Our main concern is winning this war—sir. It is very important for us not only to learn who these people are, but to find where they are getting their information from and who they are passing information to. We need Devin's help to find the top people in this ring of spies and put a stop to vital war-winning information getting to our enemies."

Morsey fingers the gold braided bands on the sleeve of his uniform. "You have not convinced me that this isn't some cock-and-bull fantasy Devin has come up with to shirk his duty. Why can't one of your own infiltrate this so-called spy ring?"

"Commander, these people have already targeted Devin. It might take us months to get someone else to find a way into this group. I have come to you today as a courtesy. I already spoke to Admiral Blaire and have been given his blessing to begin our operation. My understanding is that the *Bullshark* is at least six or eight weeks away from starting local sea trials. I hope to have this wrapped up before then."

Morsey's shoulders bunch up. "If you have the Admiral's okay I will certainly not object. You will, of course, keep me informed of your progress."

The FBI men stand to leave as Morsey remains seated, making no effort to shake hands. As they turn to leave, Walsh, the FBI man who has so far remained silent, utters under his breath, "What a prick."

Morsey pretends not to have heard the comment. Mitch, standing behind the commander, puts his hand up to cover his smirk.

With the FBI men hardly out of earshot the commander barks, "Mitch, get me the admiral's office. We'll see who has the last word here. Dismissed!"

Mitch switches on his intercom to tell the commander he has the admiral's office on the line. Pressing his hand over the mouthpiece Mitch listens to the conversation.

"Hello Al, you calling about your spy sailor?"

"Yes sir, I can't spare the man at this time, sir."

"Al, it's time for you to get with the program. I know you're pissed because you think you're being passed over. My advice is to get off the golf course and get into this war. I okayed the FBI's plan to use your man and I expect you to give them every assistance. You get my drift?"

14

"Aye aye, Admiral, I'm on it."

"Good man Al; hang tough."

Mitch waits for Morsey to hang up, then gently cradles the phone.

The FBI men with Nick stop on the stairs outside the operations building. Agent Keys offers Nick a cigarette. "I think it's best you go back to your duties with your sub; I'll square it with your captain. When we're ready to put this deal in motion I'll be back and we'll go over what we want you to do. I don't want you to talk to anyone about what we're doing. If you get hassled by your buddies about getting back late from your liberty just tell them you were drunk, okay?"

"Yeah, I guess that's best. When will we get started, sir?" Nick asks.

"Give me a coupla days, Nick. I need to get some background on what goes on here. Just go about your normal duties; if your Nazi friends are watching, we don't want to let on we're hep to 'em."

Walsh and Keys watch Nick head off to his boat. "Jerry, I want you to hop a train down to L.A. and get the low-down on this kid. Talk to his mom and dad; get to some of his friends and teachers. See if he's got some enemies and find out what they say. I'm gonna nose around here some before I go back to town."

Chapter 4

Nick leaves his last class of the day and heads to the radar shop. Carrying a laundry bag with dirty clothes, he goes to a workbench in a corner. Waiting until some of the men take a cigarette break, he ducks under the bench to place some parts that are in paper boxes into the bag. When he goes out of the building one of the men filing out of the door turns to ask him for a light. Nick nonchalantly eases the bag to the ground to light the man's smoke.

Walking quickly to the dock Nick treads gently across the gangplank to the submarine. The black painted steel of the *Bullshark* is cold to the touch with beads of moisture rolling down its sides. Nick drops down the hatch then goes to the store room and secrets his stash.

"Whatta you up to, Chief?"

Nick straightens and turns to see his shipmate posted on guard duty with a .45 Colt automatic holstered on his web belt.

"Oh hey, Biff, I'm tryin' to find something that'll take the grease stains off my pants."

"You ain't s'posed to come aboard without checkin' with me, Chief."

"Sorry, Biff. I didn't see you in the guard shack. Won't happen again."

He is lying on his back in his barracks room, reading Raymond Chandler's *High Window*, when a sailor walks to his bunk. "Captain's lookin' for you, Chief."

Nick props himself up on an elbow. "What's he want, Morris?"

"That's above my pay grade, Chief. He's in the dockside office."

Nick walks outside headed for the *Bullshark*'s tiny temporary wooden office on the dock. He carefully steps around yard workers who are busily hustling materials and tools. Welders are on the deck of the *Bullshark* adding railings and gun placements. Heavy hoses, electrical lines and steel plating snake across the deck.

Captain Shaver sits by a small desk going over a materials list with the *Bullshark*'s yeoman. Shaver is a stocky, brown-haired man in his early thirties. Scuttlebutt has it he was a football hero at Annapolis. He looks up as Nick walks in the open door.

"I've got some work for you, Chief. You can walk me over to the optical shop. Just give me a minute with the yeo."

Shaver meets Nick outside. They walk away from the dock where the *Bullshark* is dwarfed by destroyers and transport ships being completed. As they get farther toward the shops the noise of the work recedes to the point the men can talk without yelling.

"I talked to Mr. Keys, the FBI agent, Nick. I want you to know I'll do whatever I can to help. I hate the thought of spies trying to get our tech almost as much as I hate them being in our shipyards.

"Keys says he thinks you should spend as much time as you can in the radar and sound shops. I'm thinkin' that's not a bad plan. The other captains I've talked to tell me the new radar we have is the best yet, but it conks out a lot leaving 'em blind. I want you to find all the weak areas you can while you're there."

Nick's enthusiasm bubbles over musing about the new radar. "I don't know how much you've heard, Captain; we've got PPI now. That's Plan Position Indicator. You look into the screen and our boat is in the center as if you were looking down on it from above. The screen has a radial arm that sweeps around the circle. When the sweep detects an object, we can now tell its range and direction."

"Slow down, Chief, I've been to the radar school. PPI is pretty fantastic. We can really spot enemy aircraft coming at us now too, and with it's range. We've never been able to do that with the old radar. Knowing how far away the plane is now gives us time to dive. That tells me we can run on the surface more in daylight to find Jap shipping. But if the thing goes fubar we're a cooked goose."

"Sorry, Captain, this new stuff is really exciting. I've been lookin' into the problems the engineers are seein'. Faulty installation of replacement parts is a big problem. The engineers are happy to talk to anyone that speaks their language, so I've put a stash of spare tubes, condensers, and small parts I pilfered that give trouble on the boat already."

Shaver rests his hand on Nick's shoulder. "Good man. Look Nick, like I said, I'll help all I can. You're important to me and the *Bullshark*, so be careful. I want you on our first patrol."

The captain gives Nick a good natured slap on the back as he heads off down California Avenue to the huge number 680 white building, the periscope shop.

Nick crosses California Avenue to go by numbers 1 and 2 building ways where the next two submarines are under construction. The signboards on the bows of the boats are SS 414 Springer and SS 413 Spot. A bridgework of wood scaffolding surrounds both of the big fleet boats.

The dedicated yard workers are pumping out the submarines months before deadlines. He enjoys watching the men and women fit the pieces together that make up the most decorated boats in the Navy. At the bow end of the subs is building number 46. Built in 1855 this red brick building is his favorite building on Mare Island. The brickwork is finely crafted with beautiful Roman-arched windows. Nick has noticed that sailors and officers alike walking past unconsciously run their fingers down the arrow-straight mortar between the bricks.

Number 46 is in stark contrast to the huge steel-sheet sided box-like buildings that have been put up to provide work space for war production. The periscope building Captain Shaver is going to is one of the newer ones, having some 256,000 square feet of workspace.

With his classes done for the day, Nick has dinner in the cafeteria followed by a couple of beers with the other non-coms. Voices are raised from bemused veterans telling heroic tales of daring and feminine conquests to wide-eyed new recruits.

The shipyard never sleeps; bright lights push back the darkness, and the night is alive with a cacophony of sounds. Steel clangs against steel, rivets are hammered with pneumatic guns; mile-long trains deliver their loads. Brilliant sparks fly throughout the yard from electric grinders, torches, and welders. The mighty cranes rumble over their train tracks moving entire ship sections into place. Lights, high atop the cranes' skeleton-like arms, blaze out like giant monsters seeking prey.

Nick is amazed by the activity; people here are always in motion. The skill and dedication these people exhibit are akin to the fighting men on the subs they build.

Walking back to his barracks he skirts past workers off-loading a truck. The narrow alleyway is dark, the tall buildings blocking out the light. A rough voice calls out, "Hey buddy, got a light?"

Nick turns around to see two men wearing overalls with newsboy caps pulled low over their brows. He reaches in his pocket for his lighter as the men approach. One man has an unlit cigarette in his mouth. As Nick snaps the lighter open to spin the striker wheel, the second man steps in from the side to deliver a blow to Nick's stomach.

The blow is so sudden and so hard Nick doubles over gasping for breath. He is pushed to the ground; one man plants his knee down hard on Nick's back.

"The boss wants you to call him, sailor boy."

The rough-voiced man pushes a notepaper under the sailor's face.

Nick struggles to get his breath. By the time he gets up from the ground the men who attacked him are gone. He stumbles to the end of the alley holding the note to his stomach. In the light Nick reads the note; a San Francisco phone number is neatly typed on it.

Chapter 5

Agent Keys' FBI partner, Jerry Walsh, is eager to be out in the field. A younger version of Keys, Walsh has six years in the Bureau. His dark wavy hair tops a handsome face, marred a bit by a crooked nose broken as a child. He works at maintaining his athletic build, and is a confirmed bachelor. The Los Angeles FBI offices are a beehive of activity. As this is not his usual beat the agent feels lost in the hubbub.

In all the noise and confusion of the big office he has trouble concentrating trying to read the earlier Devin investigation report. He rereads the report several times to get familiar with the players. After making his decision as to who he wants to interview, Walsh begins phoning to set up appointments.

Parked on a narrow street sitting in the shade of a tree, Walsh holds up the picture of Nick Devin's mother. He gets out of the bureau's battered old Dodge as Ruth Devin comes down the sidewalk. Her hair is covered by a paisley bandana, the current badge of a working woman. She wears blue overalls with an off-white shirt, and walks purposefully, swinging a lunch box by her side.

Walsh crosses the street and tips his hat, holding his FBI identification wallet out for her to inspect. Peering at the wallet, Ruth shakes Walsh's hand.

"Hello, Mr. Walsh, I wasn't expecting you until after dinner. Our house is the next one here." Ruth opens the door and turns to Walsh. "Come on in, Mr. Walsh, make yourself comfortable. Frank will be here in an hour or so."

"I hope I'm not inconveniencing you, Mrs. Devin. We just need a little more information on your son Nick."

Ruth takes off the bandana and brushes her hair down with her hands. Walsh sees a woman who looks ten years younger than the forty-three years stated in his file.

"Your office said that Nicky is up for a new post. Frank and I know he loves the submarine service, but we both hope the Navy has a stateside job for him."

"I can't say, ma'am. My orders are to interview people that are close to him and report back. I really don't know what the Navy has in store for your son."

"I'll go start dinner. Why don't you relax and have a beer? Frank likes to have dinner ready when he gets home."

"Thank you, Mrs. Devin, a beer would be lovely. My information has you working for Warner Brother's studios, but they said you were at Clover Field today. Doesn't your husband work for Douglas Aircraft at Clover Field?"

"Ah… yes, I do work for Warner's. Do you know anything about Clover Field?"

Walsh grins. "You mean the camouflage? I read it has 5 million feet of chicken wire strung up to make the Douglas plant disappear into the landscape."

"Oh good, I was afraid to say something wrong."

Ruth smiles, her voice is both prideful and confident as she continues. "I work in the wardrobe department at Warner's; we were called on to help disguise the airfield. From the air you can't even tell the plant's there. We made miniature houses, streets, trees, cars, mounted them on the chicken wire, and hung them on poles above the plant and the field. It's so good the Douglas pilots can't find the place half the time. I was there today doing some repair work after the Santa Ana wind storm we had."

Walsh jots a note in his case book. "Your husband works at Douglas doesn't he?"

"Yes, he's a machinist there, but I can't see him when I go there because I don't have the right badge to go into his shop. You can come in the kitchen while I start dinner if you'd like. I'll make enough for you too. You may as well eat while you grill us." Walsh follows Ruth through the swinging door into the small kitchen.

"I don't want to put you out, Mrs. Devin. I know it's hard to get food with all the rationing. The questions I have are just about Nick's background. There was some kind of earlier investigation we did at the behest of the Navy."

"Well Agent Walsh, my Nicky is a very bright boy. He excels in things he calls electronics that I don't begin to understand. Frank is fascinated by that stuff too. We named Nicky after Nikola Tesla. On one of our first dates Frank scared me to death with a Tesla coil he made. The thing shot lightning out of it with a sound like thunder. I must have jumped five feet in air. It made my hair stand on end."

Walsh laughs heartily. Ruth Devin is a lady easy to be with, one who makes a person immediately comfortable. Her outgoing personality is a pleasant change from the agent's usual interviews. He sips the cold beer, enjoying the easy banter.

"Anyway," Ruth continues, "Nicky's aptitude for the science of electrics seemed to scare his Navy instructors. That's why you guys questioned us before. He knows more about some of that stuff than they do. Frank says the boy's naturally intuitive. I bet you can tell he's our only child. Stay for dinner, Mr. Walsh. When Frank gets home we can talk about Nicky all night long."

Walsh puts down his empty beer bottle. "I'd say Nick's a lucky man to have you as parents. I will stay for dinner Mrs. Devin, thank you. I haven't had a home cooked meal in a month of Sundays. I do need to run a coupla errands; I'll be back shortly."

Jerry Walsh returns toting a large cardboard box. Frank Devin answers the door.

"Come on in, Agent Walsh. Ruth said you'd be back for dinner. Can I help you with the box?"

"It's not very heavy Mr. Devin. I brought a coupla things to thank you for dinner."

Walsh takes the box to the kitchen and sets it down on a counter. Ruth and Frank look over his shoulder as Walsh pulls a bottle of Inglenook Cabernet from the box. "I hope you've got a corkscrew. I forgot to get one."

Frank rummages through a drawer to triumphantly brandish a corkscrew.

Ruth looks into the box. "My god you've got sugar and bacon. You must have murdered the butcher."

"Just a few things to make up for barging in on you. I got two small T-bones too."

Ruth brings out wine glasses from a cabinet. "It's too much, Mr. Walsh. You must have spent every ration point you have."

"I'm always on the road eating meals at diners and hotels. I had some ration coupons I wasn't going to use. So, actually, you saved me from feeling guilty about wasting some of them. I'm happier than you can imagine having a home-cooked meal."

Frank Devin busies himself tugging the cork from the wine bottle. The cork is tight, making a little "pop" when Frank tugs it out. "Shall I pour Mr. Daniel's finest, Mr. Walsh?"

Walsh turns to face the senior Devin, somewhat surprised. "You know Inglenook, Mr. Devin?"

"I know one of the finest California Cabernets ever made, Mr. Walsh. I hope you didn't think this would go to waste on heathens. Call me Frank, everyone does."

Walsh holds up his glass in salute. "Okay Frank, I'm Jerry. It's a pleasure to know people who know wine."

Frank takes a sip of his wine. "Ambrosia, Jerry." The three of them clink their glasses together.

"My father did beautiful interior wood work for some of the wineries up there. So when Ruth and I went up to Mare Island to see Nick, we pulled him away for a day and visited the Niebaum place, and some others in Napa. Pop did work for Hearst, too. Pop was a man who demanded the best of himself in his craft. He also appreciated others who strived for excellence. He liked John Daniel, the Niebaum's grandson.

The simple dinner vanishes as Nick's parents recount their son's early years to the agent.

Walsh sips the wine savoring the taste. "That was a fine meal, Mrs. Devin. You say Nick used to race jalopies. I always wanted to try that."

"Frank helped Nicky get that old Ford to run and they spent many a day repairing damage from pileups. Nicky did love running that thing. He was always trying to make it faster. His idols were Frank Lockhart and Jack Novac. Lockhart died at Daytona Beach years before Nicky raced, but his legend is still strong around here.

"Nicky met Jack Novac at a race and knew all about him. They talked about Nicky going to work for Novac's new factory in Culver City.

"Novac told Nicky that he thought electronics is going to be the future. That made Nicky more determined than ever to get a good education. He wants to go to work for Novac in the experimental lab his factory has. Apparently the lab has better equipment than anyplace on the West Coast.

"I was happy to see him stop racing so he could concentrate on college. When the war started he wanted to volunteer that Sunday. Frank and I begged him to stay in school. He enrolled in NROTC and liked the group he was in. I thought we could keep him here but he left USC to join up after his junior year.

"Even his professor was upset. He told us that he talked to Nicky, trying to get him into one of the government programs at the college that are doing war work in electronics. He said Nicky had more to offer in those programs to help in the war effort than for him to go off fighting."

Frank Devin pours more wine for Walsh. "When the boy makes up his mind I'm afraid that's it. He said he had to get in the fight. I tried to get him to at least finish school but our early losses to the Japs just seemed to burn him up. One day he comes home and says he's signed up. I was pretty mad at first. After boot camp he volunteered for submarines. He's proud to be a submariner and Ruth and I are mighty proud of our son."

Walsh finishes his wine, raising the glass in appreciation. "This has been a very nice evening. Thank you for your hospitality. I'd like to talk to some of Nick's friends and to Mr. Novac. I'll need the name of the USC professor you were talking about. I think I can finish my report with his views."

Ruth begins to collect plates from the table. "Can you really not tell us why you were sent to investigate Nicky?"

Walsh picks up his hat, turning the brim with his hands. "I'm sorry. My boss gives me an assignment and I do my job. From the information I've gotten so far, all I see is a very bright young man fighting for our country."

Frank Devin walks to the door with Walsh; they shake hands on the front step. "The professor's name is Coughlin, Jerry. Nick was a favorite of his. I think all of Nick's pals have joined up, but maybe Coughlin will know if any of them are still in school. Thanks for the wine, that's a real treat."

"Nice to have met you and the missus, Frank. Keep us in the fight."

The next day Walsh waits on the USC campus for Professor Coughlin to finish his first lecture of the morning. Sitting on a bench with his head tilted up, he enjoys the sun warming his face. The sound of a crush of students stampeding from the building arouses the drowsy agent. Mouth agape in a yawn, Walsh stretches his arms, then stands to head up the stairs into the college building.

Standing at the blackboard, Professor Coughlin has his back to the room erasing figures that look alien to Walsh. The FBI agent tilts his hat back with his thumb, furrowing his brow. Coughlin turns away from the blackboard lightly clapping his hands together to brush away the chalk dust.

"Ah, you must be the FBI man." The professor steps down from the dais to shake Walsh's hand.

Walsh proffers his I.D. "I just have a few questions about Devin, professor, and I'll be out of your hair. I am curious about the blackboard hieroglyphics."

"They are electronic symbols for different types of tubes, capacitors, transformers, and conduits used in schematics that my students need to be familiar with."

"Looks Greek to me. Did Devin get this stuff?"

Coughlin chuckles and sits down behind a student desk. "Take a pew, Agent Walsh. Mr. Devin was a most promising student, maybe the best I've come across. Wars always waste the best of the young." Coughlin raises his hands defensively.

"Don't get me wrong, I know we were attacked and that this is a war we must win. I suppose I'm still angry that Mr. Devin left. He has a natural ability to understand electricity that is rare. I believe he could have been far more beneficial to the war effort in the electronics field than fighting in the Navy, but I could not convince him of that."

"What do you think made him quit school?" Walsh asks.

"Many of the boys that were enrolled here joined right after Pearl Harbor. Mr. Devin wanted to join also. His parents and I talked him out of it. Jack Novac offered him a job at his plant doing some government projects and we thought that would do it. Then two of his friends were killed at Midway. After their deaths he could not be reasoned with."

"Do you know Novac? I was supposed to interview him also."

"I do some consulting work for him. His electronics department is involved in some very innovative projects. I understand he is in Europe doing something for our government."

"Yeah, that's what I got when I tried to set up an appointment to interview Novac. Back to Devin, why do you think he joined the submarine service?"

Coughlin turns to the blackboard then back to Walsh. "If I had to guess I would say because, from what I understand, our submarines are the most complicated war machines ever devised. That would appeal to him, or maybe the fact that it is a machine that strikes terror in Japanese mariners."

Walsh's hand hovers over his notebook. "Do you know any of Devin's friends or classmates I can talk to?"

"The list of names will not be long. Most of his male friends have enlisted."

Walsh roams the campus tracking down the people on his list.

The interior of the old Dodge is hot after baking in the sun. Walsh adjusts the vent window to dispel the interior heat that brings to mind old odors of cigarette smoke and spilt coffee. Cool air blasts his face as he accelerates down Figueroa on the way to the FBI offices.

Walsh feels as if he has shrunk two sizes in the confines of the busy office. From the telephone on his temporary desk he calls Agent Keys with his report. "Barry, I think this is a waste of time. I only found a coupla folks with anything bad to say about our boy. One guy is dyin' of envy and a Miss Anita Byrn said that Devin thought he was too good for her. The boy's clean as the driven snow as far as I can see."

Walsh glances around the office before speaking in a low voice. "Can I get outta here now?"

"Yeah, get the next train back here," Keys replies. "Things are poppin'."

Chapter 6

Barry Keys opens the door to the hotel room for Nick. The hotel on Rincon Hill overlooks San Francisco's Bay Bridge. Inside the room Nick takes in the agent's features, wondering how much to trust him.

Keys' sharp-jawed face is lined with deepening wrinkles that show his forty-one years. Shaving never seems to keep up with stubble on his cheeks. Fried food and a penchant for sweets are beginning to take their toll on his beltline. The FBI has been his beat since he left the Baltimore police force twenty years ago.

After studying the note Nick hands him, Keys says, "So from your phone call I take it you got this the hard way. At least we've got something on the guy. Make yourself comfortable. This is where we'll meet from now on. I don't want one of the bad guys to see you going into the Hunter-Dulin Building.

"Here's your key. It opens the back door that's in the alley and the door that opens to the roof. If you have to get out in a hurry, the roof gives you access to the next building to the north. That building has a fire escape ladder that will put you down on the next block. Take a look when you get a chance, just in case you need to use another exit."

Keys throws his hat on the coffee table and sits down on a faded, well-worn sofa. "I'd like to know more about your background, Nick."

"I thought you had a background report on me. What all do you want to know, Agent Keys."

"Relax Nick, call me Barry. We've got some time here and I want to get the story from you. The report I have is old and, for lack of a better description, it's colorless. What I'm looking for is how you handle yourself. The more I know about you, the more I'll be able to judge how you'll react to any situations that might arise. You understand?"

"I'm a submariner, Agent Keys, I mean, Barry. I can handle anything that's thrown at me."

Nick raises his shirt to show the bruise he got from the men in the alley.

Keys whistles. "Looks like brass knuckles did that deed. Okay, humor me, will you, Nick? Relax. We'll get to the shipyard boys. I'd really like to hear about your war patrols. I can't imagine what it must be like to live and fight in a sardine can. You can leave out the sonar and radar stuff, I wouldn't understand it anyway. You heard the admiral clear us for the war patrol info. What's it like to be depth charged?"

"Well … I'll tell you this Barry, most of the time if you're not bored to death, you're scared to death. There's nobody on a sub that's not scared at some time no matter what they say. When you're depth-charged, you can hear the ash cans splash into the water above you. You know they're coming, just not how close. Sometimes you wonder, will this be the one that gets you?

"The next sound is the thunk of the detonator and then the explosion. On my last boat I was always in the conning tower and trying to maneuver us away from the ships pitchin' the cans. Everybody is hangin' on for dear life. The boat shakes like a wet dog if the can's close. The lights get blown out so it's pitch black. Anything loose bangs around and gets under foot. Instruments and level gauges bust up throwin' glass and fluids all over; cork dust from the insulation chokes your lungs.

"We had the Japs madder than riled-up hornets after we sank two of their transports. They musta sent every can-throwin' destroyer they had. They kept us down for eight hours and dropped over a hundred cans on us. We tried every trick we could think of to get away, but they kept on us.

"If that's not enough to scare you stiff, you're in a small compartment with the watertight door dogged shut. It's over a hundred degrees, the oxygen's low and you can smell the fear and sweat of your shipmates.

"After five or six hours some of the guys said they stopped bein' scared and were either pissed off or getting bored. What they wanted more than anything was to surface and get some fresh air in the boat. The XO dropped down out of the conning tower to tell the men to shut up and quit grousing. He thought they were makin' enough noise to let the Japs know where we were.

"The depth charges are bad enough, but two of our boats were blown out of the water by our own navy destroyers and two more by our own planes. One boat took a five-inch shell right through the fairwater from one of our destroyers that didn't bother with the recognition signals.

"We're always on guard. The lookouts on duty when we're runnin' on the surface have short watches because their eyes wear out from the strain of looking through binoculars. They have to watch for enemy ships on the water, enemy planes coming out of the sun to bomb us, and periscopes on the sea's surface of enemy subs that are tryin' to sink us.

"The one thing you can depend on is the guys on the boat with you. The average age on a boat is 19. To qualify as a submariner and get your Dolphins badge, you have to be able to run every system on the boat. Our boats are the most sophisticated and complicated war machines in history. These boys can do it all. We trust each other with our lives. It only takes one mistake and the boat's lost with all hands.

"Fifty percent of the men who volunteer for submarine duty fail to qualify. You have to be in the top fifty to start training and you may not make it through training. Every submariner is the cream of the crop, Barry, the cream of the crop. On my old boat we drilled until we could dive from the surface to periscope depth in under 35 seconds. It takes every man on the boat to be on top of his job to do that."

Barry offers Nick a cigarette. "Sounds like a mighty dangerous way of fighting this war, but I get the feeling it makes the submariner a very proud man."

Nick accepts the cigarette and fire from Barry's lighter. "I'm privileged to be a submariner, Barry, and proud to fight for my country. The Japs had it all their way at sea 'til Midway, but we're doin' the damage now. Our marines are layin' 'em away at Guadalcanal after six months of unbelievable sacrifices. We've gotta keep hittin' 'em hard and get this war over with. Scuttlebutt has it the war's gonna last another five years.

"Some of the crews are flat worn-out. After four or five war patrols most guys get 30 days leave. They go home to see their parents and girlfriends. A few get married and then wonder if they want to go back to sea. They know the more war patrols you're on, the less chance you have of livin' to see your wife and family again. We're losin' a lot of boats. I don't want the Nazis or the Japs gettin' any of our technology. I want to get this war won, and soon. You tell me what you want and I'll do it."

Barry watches Nick pace the floor. Veins in the man's neck bulge with blood; you can almost see it coursing with each pulse.

"I'm a believer, Nick. I still have the feeling you're not telling me everything, but I'm with you. I hope you'll trust me at some stage and tell me what you're hiding. I don't get why our German friends would have let you go in the first place."

Nick mashes out his cigarette in an ash tray. "They don't think I'll tell the truth. They want schematics and I told 'em I could get 'em, okay?"

"It's okay as far as it goes, Nick, but why would they think you'd come back? You see where I'm comin' from, can't you? If I were runnin' this deal I'd have to have a way to keep a hold on you. It doesn't make sense that they would just let you walk."

"I don't know yet if I understand where this is going, Barry."

"I'm on your side, Nick. I'm gonna do everything I can to keep you safe. That means if I have to put my life on the line to see this though, I will. So trust goes both ways. I don't want to be blind-sided by something you think you can't trust me with. I'm fighting this war too and I've got the wounds to prove it.

"The two times I've been shot were both due to situations I got into when I didn't know where the enemy was. Think it over, Nick. I'm gonna go check in with my office and get a beer."

"Wait up, I'll go with you."

Barry stops at the door. "No, you stay here. I don't want you to be seen with me. If our Nazi pals tail you, we don't want them to see you with an FBI man. I have a woman who will use this room when we don't need it. That way, if our pals check, they'll think you come up here to get your clock cleaned. I'll bring a beer back for you."

Nick fidgets, then paces, while the FBI man is away. Squinting as cigarette smoke stings his eyes, he tries to make up his mind whether to trust the man or not. After a half a pack of cigarettes he decides, with some conditions, he will let Barry in on his problem.

Agent Keys returns with four bottles of beer in a bucket with some ice in the bottom. "Here, Nick, have a real beer. I hate that 3.2 stuff, tastes like dirty dishwater to me. I hope I gave you enough time to clear your head."

Nick takes a beer from the bucket. "I just don't want to make a big mistake here. Look if you'll promise you won't..."

"Hold up Nick, I'm not gonna make any promises 'til I know just what kind of jam you've gotten yourself into with the woman."

"What! How did you know? I mean, what makes you think it's a woman?"

"Look Nick, you're an intelligent guy, and I ain't dumb. From listenin' to you talk I don't think you'd sell out this country or your friends for anything in the world. So a twenty-one year old virile male won't talk. Not a big mystery to me. The spy ring guys we assume to be Nazis have to have something on you.

"So it's a girl you got in trouble, or the admiral's daughter, or, and I hope I'm off base here, your commanding officer's wife. I'm not here to make trouble for you or your judgments. We need to weed out these spies. So how do you think our spy friends know about your relationships?"

With a sudden lost taste for beer Nick puts down the bottle. "I didn't do any of that stuff. I met a girl at Mare Island and she is married. We have not been, what do I want to say here, um --- intimate I guess you'd say. She has a little boy that the German guy said they'd mess up if I don't get them what they want. These guys have got people at the shipyard, Barry; they seem to know everything that goes on there."

"Okay Nick. Give me her name and I'll check her out."

Nick begins to pace the room again. "That's why I've kept quiet. That's just what I don't want you to do. Those guys will know I've talked to you if you start asking questions. The only reason I'm free, and the woman and her child are okay, is that they think they have me tied up."

"Yeah, Nick, I get you. If they think you've spilled to us, they won't trust the information anyway. All right, we'll keep the girl out of it for now. I'll still need her name to do a background check. Why are you so sure these guys are Nazis?"

"Her name's Doris Wimmerman. She lives in Crockett. I'm trusting you with that, Barry.

"The reason I think the guys that grabbed me are German is that one of my professors at USC was a German who got out of the country before the Nazis clamped down on scholars. After Pearl Harbor he would sometimes imitate the Nazi bigwigs to keep us entertained. We talked after class about what Hitler was doing to Germany. The professor's accent was very much like the guys I ran into. You know, it was actually you guys that called them Nazis first."

"Yeah, okay, maybe I jumped the gun. Have you thought about what you're gonna tell the guy when you phone him? We need some time to find out more about them. I know how valuable information can be. We captured a U-boat in the Atlantic; our eggheads have found all kinds of stuff that might be helpful. You can't give any real dope but we've got to keep them interested."

Nick takes a swig of his beer before answering. "I can't get a schematic out of the shop at Mare anyway. I think I can sell the jerks that I'll have to draw a schematic from memory, a bit at a time. Hey, maybe we could feed 'em their own stuff. If we can get the radar dope from their sub, we could doctor it up and give it back to 'em."

Barry snaps a beer open from the bucket. "That's good! Yeah I like it, that's good. You've got a good head on you, man. I'll talk to Washington and see if we can get the ball rollin'. You better call the number; let's see what the guy's got to say."

Looking up at Agent Keys, Nick returns the phone to its cradle. "He wants to meet Monday on the afternoon ferry to Oakland. He says to get on early and take a seat at the back by the bulkhead. He tells me when he talks to me I'm not to turn around to look at him."

Keys stubs his cigarette out in an ash tray. "Don't get heroic, Nick. Just do what the man says. He's smart enough to get you on the ferry early on a slow afternoon and watch for anyone following you. We need to find the whole network, so don't spook the guy. Call me; but make sure you're not followed, okay? Enjoy the weekend."

"Five by five," Nick says.

Keys cocks his head. "What's that?"

"It means I hear you loud and clear," Nick replies.

Chapter 7

Nick spends the weekend back at Mare Island, which the sailors shorten to Mare or MI. He and the boat's baker, a Filipino the men call Morris, are after a Taylor ice cream machine that was destined for the wardroom of a battleship. With the captain's blessing, they barter a large ham to secure the prize. Extremely pleased with themselves, Nick and Morris go into Vallejo to celebrate after making sure the ice cream machine is safely locked away.

Monday afternoon San Francisco Bay is placid as a lake in the early September heat-wave. The sun is a brilliant ball that bursts through the fog, forcing it back to the sea. Nick wanders through the Ferry Building to wait in the sunshine at the dock for the Oakland ferry.

The ferry, pushing a small bow wave, is a two-stack side-wheeler expertly piloted to lightly nudge the dock. Stepping aside to let the tide of men and women getting off the ferry pass, Nick then waves his ticket and moves to the back of the boat. Sliding into the wooden bench seat, the rear bulkhead blocks his view.

The sun's rays coming through sea-salt frosted windows make sitting close to the window uncomfortable. Nick slides back toward the aisle where he can see the water. The air coming off the bay is cool with a salty scent.

A man, smelling unwashed, roughly pushes Nick over toward the window to sit beside him. The familiar accented voice comes from behind him.

"Pass any papers you have over your left shoulder. Do not turn around! Face straight ahead."

Feeling a knife point pressed against his side, Nick takes a breath before answering.

"I don't have anything for you yet."

The accented voice deepens, "Did you not understand my warning? The woman and the boy will be severely dealt with as will you. I want the information."

Startled upright in his seat, Nick feels a sharp pain from the knife point that pokes through his shirt.

"I can't get anything out of the shipyard; they watch you like a hawk. Look, I'll do as you say. I don't want you to hurt the woman or the boy. I have a plan to draw the radar schematic from memory. I'll take a section at a time so the drawing will be accurate. You have to understand I need to gain their trust to be able to see the schematics, it will take some time."

With a nudge to the back of Nick's head the voice says, "You will deliver the schematic to me on your next weekend liberty. There will not be any further delay. You will be under our surveillance until we meet again."

Nick feels a shift of movement behind him; without moving his head, his eyes shift hard right, straining to see the reflection in the opaque window. The blurred reflection is of the man he remembers wearing a mask the last time they met. The man's face is not clear, but clear enough so that he feels he could identify him. His knife-wielding friend does not leave Nick's side until they dock in Oakland.

Returning to San Francisco by the next ferry, Nick tries his hand at spotting a tail. He goes into a bar on The Embarcadero, orders a beer and sits at the end of the bar to watch the door. While he nurses the beer three men enter the bar at different intervals. One is a young-looking soldier, the other two look like dockhands.

The soldier and one of the dockhands pay no attention to Nick at all. The third man seems to Nick to be working hard at not paying any attention to him. The soldier asks the bartender where the action is.

"This is San Francisco, boy," the bartender replies in a booming tone. "This whole sinful city is full of any kind of action you want, but don't ask me where. I'm a Christian, get it?"

The soldier's peach-fuzzed face turns crimson. With a nervous jerk, his head turns toward Nick, who can't help smirking at the kid. Snapping his head back to the bartender the soldier flips a coin on the bar. "Yeah, I get it old man. This place ain't got nothin', that's for sure."

As the soldier exits, the bartender growls at the dockhand who has not ordered. "Hey, buddy, this ain't no library. You want a drink or what?"

All eyes of the other patrons switch from the soldier leaving to the dockhand.

"Uh yeah, gimme a beer, pal."

Nick goes to the bathroom and, on his return to the bar, finds the dockhand gone. Leaving the dim bar, he blinks in the low afternoon sunlight. Pausing on the sidewalk to light a cigarette, he takes a casual look around. The dockhand is leaning against a telephone pole gazing across the street. Nick walks back to the now-crowded Ferry Building. He stops at a cab letting off a man headed to the ferry.

The man pays the cabbie and Nick holds the rear door open, watching the dockhand scurry to cross the street. He ducks into the cab. "Take me to Chinatown." The dockhand is left at the curb. Just before Battery Street, after checking behind to see if anyone is following, he tells the cabbie to head for Rincon Hill.

Nick pays the cabbie and walks down two blocks to go behind the hotel. He enters the alley behind the hotel and waits at a shaded doorway to see if anyone enters the alley. When he is satisfied no one followed him, he unlocks the back door of the hotel and goes up to the room.

Entering the room he goes directly to the phone and calls Agent Keys. There is excitement in Keys' voice. He tells Nick to stay put, he'll be over to brief him in an hour. A little over an hour later there is a knock on the door. Nick cautiously cracks open the door to see Keys with his arms full of bags.

Keys puts the bags down on the coffee table. "I couldn't get the keys outta my pocket. I went by Blum's. Man, I love that place. I got us clubhouse sandwiches and their coffee crunch cake. We're eatin' high on the hog."

Nick grins at Keys' cheery mood. "So what's the occasion?"

Keys spreads the food out on the table. "I'll tell you, boy. I've never seen the brass move so fast in my life. I told my boss about your radar schematic plan and he phoned his boss in Washington. All hell broke loose from there. The big boss thinks this is the best thing since sliced bread.

"Have a seat and I'll tell you the whole story." Tearing into the food, Keys talks around his mouth full of sandwich.

"The story I got is that the Krauts retrieved a radar unit out of a downed British bomber. It's a centimetric unit, whatever that means. Anyway the Krauts, so my boss says, tried to make this kind of thing work and gave it up because they couldn't make it effective. So now they've got this Brit unit and they're amazed by it.

"We already have the British plans for this thing and the big boss is having a doctored schematic sent out for you to copy. The plan is for you to feed our German friends a piece at a time. My boss tells me that we have agents in place that can find out how it plays in Germany.

"So you're a hero, and I'm a hero, and everybody's happy. We're supposed to let your German friends run with it. The thought is we keep our stuff secret and let the Krauts think they've got the best stuff. After the schematic gets to Germany we can close in on the spy guys here and put 'em outta business.

"Come on, Nick, dig in. This is the best sandwich in San Francisco. Wait'll you taste this coffee cake."

Nick starts to unwrap his sandwich, "Ah, did you forget about my ferry trip?"

Agent Keys, about to take another big bite of his sandwich, slowly lowers it. "I guess I was just too excited about the big plan. So tell me, how'd it go?"

Nick chews on his first bite of sandwich before answering. "I'm pretty sure I can identify the German.

Maybe you've got an artist that could help me work up a drawing. I thought you'd be a little more interested."

"Sorry Nick, I am interested. Let's finish eating and I'll fill you in."

Barry Keys licks the coffee cake icing from the tips of his fingers. He opens his second beer then settles back in the sofa. "Blum's gotta be the best bakery in the world; I do love this city. But, as my boss says, I digress. I had a man on you from the time you came in from Vallejo. He got off the ferry in Oakland and followed the guy that sat behind you. My man watched him enter the Moore shipyard and if I don't miss my guess, we've got him on a Smith Act charge right there."

Nick sits up in his seat, some fire coming to his eyes. "Why the hell didn't you tell me you were gonna have another man there?"

"Take'er easy, Nick. I told you I'd keep you safe. What I didn't want was for you to be looking around for the man I sent to shadow you. That's happened in the past. It ruined one of my operations. My guy almost showed himself when he thought you were attacked. He said he saw you jump in your seat."

"Yeah, the yegg that sat beside me gave me a poke with his knife to show he was as tough as he smelled. It did startle me, but it didn't do any damage."

Keys laughs. "The yegg. You been readin' those detective thrillers huh? I gotta get back to the office; my guy should be calling in soon. I just wanted to celebrate a little to thank you for your help. Your idea about doctoring the dope is a hit."

Keys snaps his fingers remembering a thought. "Oh, hey, before I go, I got a submarine story for you. I read some reports ONI shared with us. You'll get a kick outta this. Seems the Kraut's radars on their subs are about useless, so their top eggheads came up with this whopper.

"They send a guy up in the air tethered to a board with a chair and an auto-gyro propeller bolted to it. Kinda like a kite. From up there he's supposed to be able to spot shipping the sub can't see. Then he radios the sub when he finds something. The report says that the guy on the board is so busy tryin' to keep the thing in the air he hasn't got time to look anywhere. If one of our planes spots the sub, the Krauts have to cut the auto-gyro guy loose to dive 'cause they can't reel him in fast enough.

"I gotta kick outta readin' that cause we keep hearin' that the Germans have the greatest scientific minds in the world. Anyway I thought you might get grin or two from it. The report's classified so if you tell your shipmates just don't tell'em where you heard it, okay?"

"That's a good one, Barry. I'll just pass it along as scuttlebutt."

Keys turns from the door, his hand on the doorknob. "What is scuttlebutt anyway? I'm askin' what the term means, do you know?"

"On the old ships it was the drinking water barrel. A butt is a barrel or cask and it was scuttled, or opened, to drink from. Sailors would gather at the barrel to spread the latest gossip. On modern ships the water fountain is the scuttlebutt."

"Very good, Nick, I learn something new every day. Keep it sharp, Nick. Call me tomorrow and I'll fill you in on the latest."

Chapter 8

Shafts of sunlight streak down though the rain clouds glinting off the still wet surfaces on Mare Island. The heavy downpour is moving to the east on a brisk wind. The hills above Vallejo are beginning to turn green, changing from the summer's golden brown.

Nick is glad to be back at the shipyard, away from the uncertainly of his FBI duties. He and Captain Shaver walk along the island's golf course, both keeping to the pathway to stay off the wet grass.

"So how much longer are you on the spy job?"

"I really don't know, Captain. Agent Keys plays his hand pretty close to the vest. I know that we have a nest of spies here and in the shipyards in Oakland. I understand that we have to try and stop these people from getting our dope, but the sooner the G-men are finished with me the better I'll like it."

"I want you on our first run, Chief. I'm tempted to ask for your release from the FBI."

"Can you give me a few weeks, Captain? I'll tell Keys we have to be done by then. I'll keep up on my duties here and only leave for the FBI stuff, no liberties."

"Okay, Chief, two weeks. I'm determined to have the best boat in the Pacific, and you're the best sound man I've ever seen. We've got a lot of new men who

47

we're going to have to drill until they're the best. All the men in the conning tower during a torpedo attack have to work together to get the results I want. My fire control party is gonna be the best we can make it. We're gonna sink a lot of Jap shipping.

"I made sure we're the first boat to get the new 5/25 deck gun, and the 40mm porch gun. I want all the new gadgets and I want you to make sure we've got the best radar and sonar units there are. I don't know if you've heard but O'Kane's boat, *Tang*, tested below 600 feet and can run over 22 knots surfaced. These Mare Island people make the best damn boats out there."

Nick snaps his lighter shut and pulls the cigarette from his mouth. "Wow, 600 feet! That's 200 better than spec. And 22 knots, man, oh man."

Shaking out another cigarette Nick offers it to the captain. Both men look out toward the shipyard, suddenly anxious to finish the fitting-out process and get back into the war.

"Captain, we can't let the Japs get that dope. If they think we can only dive to 3 or 400 feet, we've got a big advantage. They'll set their depth charges way too shallow. I'll try to speed things up, but we need to stop these spies."

"Five by five, Chief. Let's get back, and keep the info to yourself. I told you to keep you in the know."

"Thanks, sir, I won't let you down."

Shaver and Nick walk by the old coal storage buildings to the dock where the *Bullshark* is undergoing fitting-out. The captain goes into the ship's office and Nick goes aboard to watch over the work on the radar mast's motor unit.

Nick is navigating his way around the various obstacles on deck when he hears someone yell "Hey, Chief". A sailor in new dungarees walks toward him.

"Chief, there's been some twist lookin' for you. Looks kinda scrawny, thin, got short blond hair. Hope she ain't your sister. I could give you some pointers; I can wrap dames around my little finger."

Nick pushes the brim of his hat back to get a good look at the sailor. "You the new man they call lover boy? Just outta sub school, no war patrols, that right? Ask your mates who sets the watch schedules. Maybe you'll learn to mind your mouth."

Nick drops down the aft battery hatch into the crew's mess galley smiling. Morris, *Bullshark's* baker/cook, is wiping his hands on a towel.

"What's up, Cookie?" Nick asks.

"I'm makin' sure the yard boys hook up the ice cream machine so it ain't connected to our refrigeration. Captain says it can't cause a failure to the main system if it conks out. I gotta make sure it's bolted down so's it don't get lost to that ship we got it from."

Nick laughs. "Yeah, I don't know where we'd come up with another ham to get it back."

"Say there's a woman lookin' for you, Doris she said. She's been around a couple a times."

"Yeah, thanks, Moe. I'll go see what she wants at chow time. The new man, lover-boy, was just tellin' me she doesn't rate. When you see him tell him he's really pissed me off. Maybe that'll scare some a that braggin' outta him."

Later in the day, Nick walks into the printing office where Doris Wimmerman sits almost hidden behind her clacking typewriter. Her short blond hair hangs straight down with bangs at her face. The large-framed round glasses she is peering intently through give her an owlish appearance. With her brow furrowed in concentration her small pale fingers hunt over the keyboard. Nick raps on the counter to gain Doris' attention.

Doris' hands fly up to her glasses in an effort to focus on the man at the counter. Her face lights up, unwrinkling from her startled expression.

"Nick, Nick, I'm so happy to see you." Her face becomes serious; she looks to her right, then lowers her voice. "We have to talk. I'll go check out for lunch."

Doris checks out at the time clock and motions Nick to follow her. They walk to the interior of the building to a stairway and up two flights of stairs. She turns back to Nick and whispers, "There's an office at the end of the hall where we can talk. The men that work there are out for the day and don't lock up when they leave."

Doris closes the door behind them and clenches Nick in a hug. "Where have you been? I've been desperate; you said you'd help us. Nick, they've got Benny. Two men came and took Benny away with them. One of the men told me you wouldn't give them what they want."

Nick feels Doris' body begin to tremble with sobs, her fingers digging in to him.

Nick pulls back to look into Doris' eyes. "I can't get the stuff they want yet, but I will. I won't let them hurt Benny. We'll get Benny back."

"Where do you go, Nick? You're never here when I need you. Please, you need to tell where you'll be; I'm so alone here. Do you have a woman somewhere, is that where you go?"

"I don't know where I'll be most of the time, so there's no way I can tell you. You know I have training classes I have to attend, but I also have to do the captain's bidding. He sends me out with a list of things he wants for the boat."

Doris, sniffling, dabs her eyes with her handkerchief. "You didn't answer my question."

Nick turns away from Doris to walk toward the windows at the back of the office. "Right now we need to think of a way to get Benny."

Hands on his hips, Nick stands in front of the window looking out toward Mare Island Strait. Ships, boats, lighters, and tenders of every size and shape line the docks. Two, and in some places, three or more ships are moored together getting the finish work done. Only small patches of sun-speckled water peek through.

Nick's mind wanders to his new boat and how easy it would be to just be concerned with getting the fitting-out done and sailing away. His musing is shattered by the shrillness in Doris' voice.

"Nick what do we do? I have to call the man with your decision as soon as possible."

"Where did they abduct Benny?" Nick asks.

Doris tugs at strands of hair by her ear. "What do mean?"

"Where was Benny when the people took him?"

Doris moves to stand by Nick at the window. "He was home; they took him from home."

"Okay, tell 'em I'll bring a drawing if they return Benny to your house tonight."

Doris circles her arms around Nick's waist. "Oh thank god. I've been worried sick; thank you, Nick. I'll do whatever you want to make it up to you."

"There's nothing you need to do for me, Doris. Give me the address of your house; I'll see you there by nineteen hundred hours."

Doris clutches Nick's arm. "I'm so alone here. I'm so afraid of those men and what they'll do to Benny. Please stay with me awhile. Talk to me. Tell me about your boat, your patrols, anything to get my mind away from this awful fear. Please Nick."

Nick turns to Doris, grim-faced. "If I have to leave the base tonight I have a lot to do before I can leave. I've got to go, Doris. I'll try to be early tonight, we can talk more then."

Dabbing a handkerchief to her eyes, Doris turns away. Nick lightly touches her trembling shoulder before leaving the room.

Captain Shaver bangs his fist on the desk. "Goddamn it, Devin. Didn't you just tell me there would be no more liberties?"

"I'm sorry, sir. I meant that I wouldn't take my regular days off. This is really serious or I wouldn't ask. Captain, I'm having a hard time with this. I don't mean to whine. I would far rather concern myself only with our boat; I want to be back in the fight. It isn't right that I can't tell you what's happening. If it will help I'd like to have Agent Keys fill you in."

"Yeah, I'd like to talk to Keys again, Chief. We need to set up some ground rules and a time limit. Can you call him from here?"

"I can try sir, but I don't know how he'll take it. He might get his back up and tell me he can't talk with anyone else listening."

Shaver slides the phone across his desk toward Nick.

Agent Keys' jaw muscles ripple as he tightens his grip on the phone. "Why the hell are you callin' in front of your captain? Damn it, man, didn't you listen to me? Listen good. Your captain's got no pull here. I can take you off your boat for the duration if that's what I need to close this case. Put your captain on the phone."

"Captain Shaver, before you start, I'm askin' you not to threaten me with any ultimatums. I have Admiral Blaire's blessing to use Devin any way I see fit."

Keys changes the phone to his right hand and rubs his ear. "Captain, I apologize for being rude. I need to find out why Nick called from your phone. If you'll let me speak to him privately, I promise to hear you out."

Shaver, obviously displeased, hands the phone to Nick and tells the yeoman to follow him to the *Bullshark*.

Keys sits back in his chair. "Okay, look Nick, sorry I yelled at you. I know you must have a good reason, so what's the deal?"

Nick tells Keys about the abduction of Doris' son, and how he needs to get a radar schematic to get the boy back.

"I see the problem but you shoulda called me first before you promised a schematic. We haven't gotten the dope from Washington yet. I understand that you want to help your friend, but let me make this very clear. You are not to give the enemy any information that has not been cleared by the Bureau and the Navy. Do not take any drawings from Mare Island."

Nick sits down heavily. Running his hand over his face he stares without seeing. Keys' voice booms out of the phone. "Nick, are you there?"

Startled, Nick replies, "I'm here, Barry. I'm trying to think of something I can do. I won't give the enemy anything that will hurt us. I won't sell out for anything but I need to try and save the boy."

Squeezing the phone to his ear with his shoulder, Keys shuffles papers on his desk trying to find an old magazine article he found on radar. "Nick, I've got a rudimentary diagram from a science magazine that shows an antenna, with lines drawn to a receiver, then to a processor and then to a display. It's from the early thirties to show how radio waves could be harnessed to find airplanes."

"Yeah, I know what you mean, there's one on the wall at my radar class. That's not what they're after, Barry."

"I know, Nick, but we don't have the right dope yet; so sell 'em something simple. Tell 'em that's all you've got for now until you can get a look at the latest schematics. Draw the diagram in front of them, then sign it. That's proof that you're gonna deal with 'em. Tell 'em they could hang you with that drawing if you don't play ball.

"Good luck, Nick. Let me know how it goes. You can put your captain back on the phone now."

"It'll take me a minute to get him back to the phone, sorry, Barry."

"Stay sharp, Nick. There's nobody better than you to sell this deal."

Chapter 9

Captain Shaver puts the phone down and looks up at Nick. "Okay I get it. Damn it the guy's right; you're right, we've got to get these guys. Nobody's safe with those rotten spy bastards loose. I guess I'm just worried about getting back to our business with the Japs. But I'm more worried about Keys pulling you off permanently; he's got the admiral's blessing.

"The guys that have been on leave are coming back on duty. Now that they've had time to think, it's hard for them to commit to getting back to the war. I've been best man at two of our officer's weddings here at Saint Peter's Chapel.

"We get to thinking of the narrow escapes we've had; the depth charging, the Jap Betty's dive bombing us, destroyers trying to ram us. The guys keep saying the more patrols we go on the less chance we have of coming back to our families. And now we get word that Mush Morton and the Wahoo are lost. Everyone here at the yard loved the man; he's legendary.

"But I'll tell you something: what I'm thinking is, we've got the best boat ever to take the fight to the Empire and come home. I just want to get to it. Stop thinking of the negatives and get on with the job. Once we're on patrol I'll make sure there's no time for anyone to think of anything but the boat and doing the best job we can. So go get those bastards, Nick."

Devin walks to his barracks to change clothes with his mind spinning overtime. The room he shares is empty and seems strangely quiet, as if totally detached from the hustle outside. Nick lies down on his bunk with his hands behind his head. The last war patrol he was on with the old *USS Bayfish* springs vividly into focus.

The captain of the *Bayfish*, Arthur Diggs, was a stern, almost mirthless man. What he may have lacked in personality he more than made up for with his aggressive attacks on Japanese shipping.

After radar contact with a Japanese convoy the captain ordered flank speed to intercept. They ran on the surface which was a dangerous thing to do in daylight. However the sub was much faster on the surface; its four big diesel engines snarling raucously drove the boat hard through the sea. The bow cleaved the sea leaving a roiling wake of white water.

They closed on the convoy of five ships guarded by three destroyers. Three of the merchant ships were tankers, low in the water, filled with gas or oil. A very plum target. Captain Diggs raced his boat ahead of the convoy to set up his attack. With the darkness of night approaching he would submerge to line up his shots.

When the convoy appeared there were not three, but actually four destroyers running interference. The Japanese were alert and searching; sonar pings sounded loud inside the hull of the *Bayfish*. It was almost as if they knew the *Bayfish* was staging an attack. The bong, bong, bong, of general quarters sounded. Battle stations, torpedo rooms stand ready, sounded through the ship.

They could not get a shot with the destroyers in the way. The captain maneuvered the submerged *Bayfish* under one of the destroyers and set up his attack on the first tanker in line. At a distance of 1500 yards to the tanker, he planned to fire a spread of three torpedoes at the first tanker and three more at the next one following.

The captain used very short sightings with the periscope to avoid detection and called out firing instructions. The periscope was raised, the captain took bearings in an instant, then the periscope vanished back down under the sea.

Nick took in all the sounds through his sonar earphones. He patted his knee with his hand to count the swishes of the tanker's propellers to confirm the tanker's speed. As the heat in the 8 by 12-foot conning tower rose, all 12 of the men in the small space dripped with sweat.

The hours of tracking the enemy and forming a firing solution came to a head. "Fire One," the captain called. At ten-second intervals two more torpedoes were on the way. Seconds, that seemed like hours to the crew, ticked by before the first torpedo found its mark. A huge blast rocked the submarine; the tanker must have carried aviation fuel. The night was brilliantly lit with a fireball that reached thousands of feet into the air.

The sheer intensity of light caused the captain to flinch away from the periscope's eye piece. Nick called out "Destroyer's high speed screws headed right for us, Captain."

The bright light let the Japanese destroyer's crew follow the wakes of the torpedoes right back to the *Bayfish*. "Take her down fast, right full rudder," the captain called out. "Rig for depth charge, rig for silent running." There would be no chance for another shot now. The crew instantly knew they were in for a beating.

Nick snatched the earphones off his head. "She's dropped a load of ash cans!" The splashes were heard through the hull of the submarine. WHAM, WHAM, WHAM, WHAM. *Bayfish* convulsed violently, hydraulic piping throughout the hull shook so hard it rang. Chunks of cork insulation fell, ripped from the interior of every compartment. The executive officer grabbed the periscope cable to keep from falling. He regained his balance and pulled his red swollen hand away.

The violence of the ash can explosions whipped the periscope cable so hard it almost broke the XO's wrist. He looked around sheepishly in the dim light to see if anyone noticed. Captain Diggs grinned coolly at the XO, shaking his head.

The sub tilted down sharply at the bow, trying to pull as much sea water over her as possible to shield her from the attackers. Nick pulled the earphones back to his head. "I've got four DE (destroyer escort) screws now, Captain. I think they're trying to box us in."

For fourteen hours the destroyers ran a deadly pattern over the *Bayfish*. One DE dropped a load of depth charges, then stood off while another DE listened with her sonar gear for noises from the sub. The captain waited by Nick's shoulder to learn where the DE's were and tried to slip the boat away.

Some sailors were quiet, alone with their thoughts. A few stared blankly, braced for the next explosion, wondering if this one was the one that would kill them. Others went about their tasks as quietly as possible. One man in the forward torpedo room calmly painted a Japanese flag on the door of the torpedo tube that sank the tanker.

With the sub rigged for silent running, none of the ventilating fans, bilge pumps, or air conditioning could be run. Temperature in the boat rose past 125 degrees, the humidity was stifling. In the after engine room, water rose from small leaks caused by the depth charge pounding. The engine room gang formed a bucket brigade to dump the water in the after torpedo room. Water had to be kept from the electric motors at all costs.

At eighteen hours of almost constant pounding the men were growing lethargic. There was no longer enough oxygen to keep a match alight. Men were bathed in their own sweat. The crew sprinkled CO_2 absorbing powder down to combat the rising carbon dioxide level, then gulped salt pills to replace their sweat depleted systems.

Without the air conditioning running, the ship sweated too; every vertical surface ran with rivulets of condensation. The next load of ash cans were very close; shattered instrument gauges sent glass flying, lights went out all over the boat. High amperage electrical circuits shorted in the humidity and sent sparks arcing, the sailors groped in the darkness to repair damages. The hours of drilling for emergency repairs was paying off handsomely as men went calmly and quietly about their work.

Nick and Diggs tried every trick they had learned to find an escape route. The water they were taking on made it difficult to maintain depth control. They jinked to different headings only to find one of the Japanese DE's already there boxing them in.

After hours of running solely on battery power, Captain Diggs huddled with his fire control party. "They're trying to make us surface. If we stay down much longer we're gonna run out of juice. I'm gonna try to get us free, but if we don't get away this time we're gonna battle surface while we've still got maneuvering power and fight it out."

Knowing this tactic would be almost certain death, Diggs ordered the XO to go quietly through the ship and tell the battle surface men to stand ready.

Captain Diggs stood next to Nick. Both men had been on duty for over 40 hours. Nick cocked one of his ear phones out so the captain could hear also. Another DE started his run. "Captain, when this guy comes at us we could try running right under him at max speed. The other DE's can't hear us with all the noise and we may be able to break out if an ash can doesn't get us."

The captain ran his hand over his stubbled cheek. He weighed the idea for only an instant before making his decision. "Okay. Where are the other DE's?"

"If we turn to starboard under this DE it will put two of the others to aft port and the other one off the port bow, sir." The captain ordered a turn to starboard. The boat was a little sluggish to respond. Suddenly Nick raised his hand. He pulled the other ear piece over his ear and pressed both earpieces against his head. "Sir, the port bow DE is shifting away from us! This is our best chance to get away."

The captain issues urgent orders: "Rudder amidships, emergency flank speed."

Eyes of the eleven men of the fire control party were on Nick as he turned on the wheel above the sonar console. More charges exploded, reverberating through the hull but with much less force. Nick turned on his seat to face the crew. "We're away Captain. I can make out three DE's; I don't where the fourth guy went. The remaining DE's are throwing cans all over the place. They've lost us."

Diggs wipes the sweat from his face with a handkerchief. "Secure from emergency speed. Stay at flank. Take us up to 64 feet."

For the first time anyone aboard could remember, the captain displayed a real emotion: he clapped Nick on the shoulder. "Good job, Devin, damn good job, man."

A cheer went up. Diggs addressed the crew over the intercom to tell them they were on the way to the surface, and to secure from battle stations. The entire ship rang with cheers. Bilge pumps immediately went online. The ship's stewards soon passed coffee and sandwiches up to the conning tower.

At 64 feet the captain ordered the periscope up. He swung the scope 360 degrees then steadied it aft. "The DE's are milling around back there throwing cans like a bunch of mad hornets. Steady on this course, helmsman. We'll put another 2000 yards on before we surface."

After the air pressure that had built up in the boat was bled off, the conning tower hatch was opened to welcome the cool evening air. The first diesel engine fired, sucking air from the open hatch through the boat.

The captain ordered a thorough radar search before allowing the men their dose of depth charge medicine. The pharmacist's mate handed out the brandy after which the men who wanted to could come on deck in alternating groups to enjoy the night air.

There were a few sailors aboard that swore to stay below deck until the war patrol was completed. This patrol would last for 52 days. Whether this was from superstition, or a contest to see who was toughest, few men endured it. The rest of the fifty-odd enlisted men who were not at a duty station below were glad to be on deck. One sailor found ash can shrapnel wedged in the teak wood foredeck. The rear-mounted four-inch deck gun also bore scars from torn metal.

With that much shrapnel littered on the boat, the deck crew, and soon everyone on the boat, knew they had come very close to "buying the farm".

Chapter 10

Coming awake, Nick bolted straight up in his bed. The room was far too big to be on the *Bayfish*. He shook his head trying to clear the memory. He couldn't escape, even now, in the safety of his Mare Island barracks. He had smelled the diesel oil, the tang of the dark sea, and felt the tension of the other men in the conning tower. The thoughts of his last war patrol on the *Bayfish* were too strong. He couldn't resist thinking back to the dangers and excitement of that patrol. As soon as Nick lay back resting his head on the pillow his eyelids grew heavy. With sleep came a return to the *Bayfish*; his dream put him back into a continuation of the same war patrol.

Three days after the depth charge attack had faded, the monotony of normal duty returned. The seas were calm and no Japanese shipping was sighted. Nick slept soundly in his bunk on the *Bayfish*; no dreams spoiled his rest. The sounds and the motion of the boat assured his body and mind all was well.

A voice that seemed far away drifts into his head, his body shakes, his eyes snap open: a sailor is shaking him awake.

"Captain wants you in the conning tower ASAP, Chief." Nick was up in a flash, sprinting to the narrow ladder and up into the conning tower.

Captain Diggs herded the radar operator away from the set to make room for Nick. "What do you make of this image, Devin?"

Nick sat in front of the scope's screen to see a ghostly green blob wobble. Diggs leaned over Nick's shoulder as the cursor passed the image again.

It only took an instant for Nick to flip a switch shutting off the radar.

"It's a lower power radar unit, Captain. I'd say a Jap sub looking for air traffic. I don't think they could detect us, but they could home in on our radar."

"Did you get range or course?" Diggs asked.

"Range five-oh-double-oh, sir, I think two-eight-oh course. I can verify with short bursts of our radar without letting him spot us." Nick powered the radar, took the bearing and shut it off. "Target bearing two-six-oh now, sir."

Diggs ordered battle stations; his ship could now be hunter or hunted. Diggs never hesitated: he was the hunter, the Japanese submarine his prey. The captain climbed the ladder to the bridge; the lookouts scanned the inky black night. "Keep a sharp eye, boys. There could be more than one of 'em."

Everyone aboard the *Bayfish* knew the Japanese sub could easily turn the tables. Just one of those Japanese torpedoes with their thousand-pound warheads would blow the *Bayfish* apart. There would be no survivors.

Diggs scanned the darkness, straining to find a break between a horizon and the sea. Leaning over the bridge speaker he barked an order. "Devin, I want you on sonar. It's too black up here to see anything. We're gonna run hard to get ahead of him from his last course heading. When we've reached the area I want the ship's engines stopped so you can pick up any sounds."

Hours later the captain ordered the ship's engines stopped. "You're on, Devin." The executive officer squeezed Nick's shoulder. Nick raised his hand with the okay sign, already listening hard. The boat was eerily still until metal banged against metal below deck. Nick shook his head, the XO barked into the ship's intercom. "Belay that noise! All stations secure from any racket."

Tension in the conning tower was as heavy as the night was black. Men in the boat sat quietly; the galley was full of men drinking endless cups of coffee.

"I've got screws," Nick exclaimed. The XO relayed the message to the captain. "Course still two-five-oh, speed 10 knots, he's not zig-zagging. He'll be two-five-double-oh yards off our bow on this course. Our radar has him now, sir. He's searching with his radar."

"Secure our radar," Diggs snapped. "Only make short sweeps."

Bayfish sat still in the water, silently waiting for her unsuspecting prey to cross her bow. Diggs ordered battery power to close the distance; he wanted the Jap sub at less than 1500 yards before firing his torpedoes.

Diggs was on the target-bearing transmitter, peering through the binoculars trying to locate the enemy submarine. "Where is he, sound?"

Nick answered quickly. "He's drifted to his left, sir."

Diggs, in a cool firm voice, ordered, "Radar, get me a bearing! Torpedoes forward, we're firing a three-torpedo spread."

The man on the torpedo data computer got the radar bearings and spun the dials to get a firing solution. Range was now 1800 yards. Diggs wanted to be closer but didn't want to lose his chance. He ordered the torpedoes fired. Everyone watched the second hand of the clock tick. The hand made one complete round. At the second round the captain's voice filled with disgust came over the intercom. "What the hell happened? We missed with all three?"

The radar operator powered up the scope, then told the exec that the Jap sub increased speed by a few knots. The torpedoes would have all missed her going astern.

Nick called out, "She's diving, I can hear her ballast tanks filling."

No one knew if the enemy sub understood she was fired upon. The enemy could now be lining up the *Bayfish* for a torpedo attack. Now was the time to clear the area.

But not Diggs; he was like a dog with bone in his teeth. "All ahead full, right full rudder! Plot that bastard's course and give me a speed. We're gonna run ahead of him again and wait for him to surface. I don't know why he went under but I don't think he knows for sure we're after him. The man seems kinda lackadaisical to me, or just doesn't know his business."

At the plotting station in the conning tower the XO swore under his breath, "What speed does an enemy sub have submerged? Six knots, eight, ten, hells bells

I'll make it the greatest distance. Diggs will kill me if the guy gets by us."

The captain wanted to be bow on to the enemy sub. This was the perfect set-up for firing, and if the Japanese sub were aware of them, it gave the smallest target for the enemy sub to shoot at.

Bayfish's four huge diesels snarled, powering her to meet her prey. If the Japanese captain dived as a precaution, he'd come up for a look see before too long. Diggs figured the enemy sub would surface within a couple of hour's time. The torpedo men finished inspecting and reloading the forward tubes. Once the sleek American sub reached the plotted station all compartments fell silent.

Nick thought of his shipmates below the conning tower; he knew there would be a lot of scuttlebutt about who was hunter and hunted. In the conning tower he had first hand information; below an interminable wait was the sailor's lot. He snapped his head up, back in focus. After what seemed an eternity, Nick turned to the XO, "I've got noise bearing zero-one-four."

"Put it on the speaker," the XO ordered.

Nick flipped the switch. A rushing sound filled the small compartment. The sound grew, then, with a clank, the sound ended. The exec shouted into the bridge mike, "She's blown tanks, Captain. It'll be up soon at zero-one-four."

Diggs ordered a dive and followed the watchmen down the ladder. He was not going to take a chance of being detected. Sliding silently under the sea, the deadly game of cat-and-mouse was coming to a head. Diggs peered through the periscope. The enemy sub was going to cross the *Bayfish*'s bow without a care, still not zig-zagging. Diggs ordered to close the range; he would not miss this time.

Each time the periscope went up Diggs called out the bearings. The XO began to fidget; he badly wanted to yell fire one. What's the skipper waiting for? Diggs ordered the periscope up; he would not be rushed. Now Diggs knew he had the enemy cold! Bearing mark! Set! Fire! At ten second intervals three torpedoes were away. Diggs followed the wake of the first torpedo. The conning tower clock ticked, eyes watched the slim red hand twitch.

A boom of explosion slammed against the *Bayfish*'s hull, then a second. Diggs saw the enemy sub broken amidships, the two pieces formed an inverted V as it sank beneath the sea. No one would get out. Horrible sounds of a ship dying were heard by all aboard the *Bayfish*. The men cheered, elated by the death sounds of the enemy sub breaking up on her way to the bottom of the sea.

The continuing sounds of the enemy sub's compartments collapsing under the sea's unrelenting pressure caused the ship's company to become subdued. The tortured steel continued to screech as if in agony. The *Bayfish* sailors realized they had killed one of their own kind. It could have been them struggling against the icy depths stealing their last breaths.

Diggs spoke into the intercom. "We're outta fish, and headed for the barn. Pearl Harbor and the Royal Hawaiian await. Good job and well done to every one of you. I'm proud to serve with you." A loud cheer broke out in every compartment.

Chapter 11

Nick got up from his Mare Island bunk to wash his face. His dream was so vivid that when he got up he thought he could feel the *Bayfish* move beneath him. Splashing cold water on his face, he looked up into the mirror above the wash basin. Checking his watch he was amazed so little time had passed. Time to dream is over; Crockett will be an altogether new experience in containing fear.

Crockett is a small town that sits beneath hills that rise high above the Carquinez Strait. The huge sugar refinery, the town's lifeblood, is situated on the water's edge. The town became nationally famous for the union wars in the late thirties that left the streets running with blood.

Tires on Nick's bus hum over the metal grating sections of the tall steel bridge that spans the water. Stepping off the bus Nick follows Doris' instructions and climbs up the steep First Avenue to a small clapboard house perched atop the hill. Doris opens the door before he can lift his hand to knock. Her face is marred by a dark bruise under her right eye.

"They didn't bring Benny back," Doris wails.

From inside the house a rough voice yells, "Get away from the door, you stupid girl."

Nick storms past Doris only to be met by the fist of the same odorous man from the ferry. He stumbles backward toward the open door. The man who hit him grabs Nick's shirt front to pull him back into the front room.

"Shut that damned door, you idiot," Nick's assailant shouts.

Doris scrambles meekly to the door to pull it closed.

Nick regains his balance and swings a roundhouse punch that just catches the tip of the man's chin. The man tries to wrap his arms around Nick to ward off more punches. They tumble to the floor rolling over each other trying to gain an advantage.

Doris' screams bring a second man out of a back room on the run. He pulls a leather sap from his back pocket and brings it down hard on Nick's head.

Nick stirs back to consciousness with Doris holding a wet cloth to his head. He realizes he is bound to a chair at the kitchen table.

"Nick, please do not make trouble. You must obey these men. I'm afraid for Benny; please give them what they want."

A voice from behind says, "Yeah, that's right, bright boy, give us what we want. Where's the plans you're supposed to have?"

The two henchmen move into Nick's field of view. Both men, Nick thinks, are the same ones he saw wearing masks in San Francisco. The man he hit when he came in is the taller of the two men. He is heavy set, unshaven, unwashed, and appears to be somewhat dull. The slightly shorter man is neater, very pale, and the same man Nick saw trying to follow him on The Embarcadero.

"The boss told you to bring the radar information. Where is it?" the pale man asks.

Nick balls his fists and pulls against his bonds. "You bastards must be real proud, kidnapping children and beating up women. What makes low-lifes like you sell out your country? Are you too scared to go to war and fight?"

The man who slugged him at the door hits Nick again, splitting his lip.

"You want more, sailor boy? I can do this all day."

The other henchman pushes the hitter aside. "Stop it, Dieter, the boss wants the radar plans. Alright kid, where's the dope? Do I have to bring you one of the boy's eyes, or do you have the dope?"

"No, you heroes don't have to hurt the boy. Our eggheads have a brand new system. They haven't even sent the latest schematics yet. You can check with your people at the shipyards. The reason I came here is to draw you a basic parts diagram to show I'm gonna cooperate. Give me some paper and a pencil and I'll get to it."

"The boss told you to get the plans and have 'em here today."

"Your boss," Nick says, "is gonna want the latest unit that we're gonna have on our boats. If I give you the old dope he's gonna think I'm tryin' to trick him. Untie me and let me give you what I have. I'll sign the drawing so that you'll have me for treason if I ever try to double-cross you."

"Dieter, untie our friend here," the man says, pulling a revolver from his pocket. "Woman, get him something to draw on."

With his hands free, Nick wipes blood from his mouth.

Doris brings a tablet and pencil to the table. "Nick, I'm so sorry. We'll be okay if you just do what they ask."

"Didi, get the woman outta here."

"Yeah Didi, but keep your dirty hands off her," Nick snarls.

Dieter smacks the back of Nick's head.

"You touch Doris or me again and I'll bust your head in. You guys are gonna have to bring your boss to any future meetings. I don't think you're bright enough to think on your own."

Dieter's face contorts with hatred as he advances on Nick. Raising his pistol to bear on Dieter, the second henchman yells out, "Dieter! I told you to get the goddamned woman outta here. I'll take care of the sailor boy.

"Okay, start drawing. If this is a trick I'll make you watch while Dieter messes up the boy and his mother. He likes his work."

Nick picks up the pencil. "I told you I'd cooperate. If you harm the boy or Doris all you'll have is this drawing. I may not be willing to sacrifice the boy or the woman but I'll die for my country. You tell your boss that. The next time we meet, you have your boss be there or you won't get anything further from me, get it?"

"Who the hell do you think you are? I'm givin' the orders here. You do what I tell you to do, get it? I hate smart punks like you. I'd just as soon put a bullet in that big brain you're supposed to have."

Nick goes back to work on the drawing. "That would get you nothing. I'm drawing but don't think I have to like it."

Finishing the drawing, Nick signs the bottom of the paper and pushes it across the table to the man with the pistol.

The man looks over the paper keeping the pistol trained on Nick.

"That's it? That's all you got? A dozen boxes with arrows goin' one to the other. I don't think the boss is gonna be amused. What's the funny squiggles supposed ta mean?"

"The squiggles are electronic symbols. Either your boss or someone with brains will know what it means. You have classified war material with my signature on it."

"Okay, bright boy, get the hell outta here. Boss says for you to stay on the yard 'til you hear from us."

Nick gets out of the chair with the muzzle of the pistol following him up. "I go where the Navy and my captain tell me to go."

"I got a bullet with your name on it, boy. You got any notion a' messing with us I'm itchin' to put one in ya. Get goin'."

As Nick turns and walks out of the kitchen he hears the gunman's chair scrape against the floor behind him.

"Don't stop, boy, there ain't nothing more for you here. Go on out the door and back to the shipyard. You'll be hearin' from us."

Nick goes out of the front door and stops at the bottom of the steps. Night has fallen; across the river below he sees the work lights blazing on the Mare Island Shipyard. To the east, the city of Vallejo's lights blanket the rolling hills. Along the riverside a long train clacks across the rails; the familiar and somehow soothing whistle sounds at an intersection as it pulls its load west to Richmond. Nick balls his fists in frustration and walks down the hill.

Chapter 12

A wet fog swirls as it rises above the long buildings alongside the wharves at Fort Mason. It is just high enough to see hundreds of soldiers boarding a transport ship. Lines of GI's, heavy with brand new equipment and backpacks, seem endless. John Smith, who's real name is Amil Seidel, is lying prone on top of a building off Laguna Street, peering though a high-powered telescope. From this location he can watch the naval traffic on the Bay as well as army movements at the Fort.

This is but one of the places he has on both sides of the Bay to spy on America's war effort. He keeps his well-funded spy ring small and rarely meets his minions in the same place. In the first months of the war the FBI rounded up a large number of German spies. Most worked out of German embassies and had been under surveillance by the FBI for quite some time.

Seidel stayed away from the embassies before the war erupted. He was then a very small cog in the German spy scheme. After the FBI arrests, Seidel became a last-ditch effort by Berlin to gain military information in San Francisco.

Amil came to America to fast-track his dream of becoming an acclaimed stage actor. He had a good command of English and projected his voice well. However, no one in New York was capable of recognizing what he thought was his massive talent. Seidel thought movie actors had little talent, but this could be his last chance at stardom. Reluctantly, he boarded a train for the Promised Land. Hollywood, it seemed, also had no use for his talent.

Becoming dejected and desperate, he devised a grand scheme of spying on the Southern California military build-up before the war. Using every contact he knew, Seidel finally found a German ear. Berlin's decision was one he knew well; don't call us, we'll call you. Down to his last nickel, he, at last, discovered his dubious talent.

Gaining entrance to a big Hollywood party, Amil charmed society women with his stories of wealth and lands lost by the Nazi takeover in Germany. He, a wealthy count, escaped the Nazi menace by supreme heroics with only the shirt on his back. Subterfuge, combined with his newly fostered hatred for everything American, was now his driving force.

Defrauding a rich widow of her estate, Amil fled to Mexico City to enjoy his wealth. Unfortunately, Seidel had not counted on the rich widow's son who tracked him down to his rented Mexican villa. The son and his friends delivered a brutal beating to Seidel before leaving with all the money he stole from the old widow. Destitute again, he was forced into menial labor by his tough Mexican landlord to pay his debts.

Soon after Germany declared war on America, Seidel contacted Berlin. With most of their spies compromised, Berlin needed information. A deal was struck; Germany would pay off Seidel's debts so he could manage commercial properties around the San Francisco Bay area. Some of the properties were already in Berlin's possession with clear titles.

Seidel's main contribution was his conduit to Berlin. He became a silent partner in a North Beach restaurant. Some game fish and produce came to the restaurant from Mexico. Seidel used this conduit as his sole communication to Berlin. After being in the spy business for two years, Seidel came to believe he was too clever for the American FBI.

Indeed, his paranoia of phones and contacts did keep him safe from the FBI's spy sweeps. He promised Berlin great things; he would deliver not only military movements but also America's greatest technical secrets.

His plan to obtain America's radar secrets was his most daring and auspicious to date.

Chapter 13

The two henchmen, Willi, the pale man, and Dieter, the strong-armed dullard, knew they were in trouble when the boss ordered them to the Chinatown meeting. This was the place they took Nick after Freda drugged him. As far as they knew, there was only one entrance and exit. The boss told them if they tried to find another exit through the warren, one of the Chinese tongs would kill them. It was a place Willi hated to go.

Willi leads the way down an alley through a concealed opening between two buildings. They carefully walk down the uneven steps to a lower level. There are a few naked low-watt light bulbs hanging by their cords that barely illuminate their pathway. Willi has no idea how far underground they are. He hates the musty moist dirt smell; it makes him feel as if he is walking into his own grave. A flashlight in his pocket is the only protection to combat the fear of the lights going out which would serve to complete his terror.

After passing several heavy-looking wooden doors, the narrow passageway takes on a sickly sweet chemical odor. Trudging deeper into gloom, they finally stop at a door painted green with a gold border. Willi pushes a button by the door three times short, one long. The door silently glides open to reveal a room that is no more than twelve feet square with a low ceiling. Seidel earlier told them that the room was completely soundproof.

The boss sits behind an ornate table as the two henchmen enter. They both suspect that the boss' gray moustache and hair are a disguise. A Luger pistol on the table is close by his right hand.

Willi takes his hat off, holding it in his right hand. "Uh, you wanted to see us, boss?"

"Sit down!" Seidel commands. Both henchmen scramble to the two chairs facing the table.

Waving Devin's drawing, Seidel asks, "Now tell me how you came to accept Devin's drawing. Wilhelm, you know this is not what I want."

"It's like I said in the note, boss. He said they've got a new system coming. He said you'd want the new stuff and would think he was tryin' to trick you if he didn't get the one they're gonna put in his sub."

"You did tell him there would be a grim consequence if he does not cooperate, did you not?"

"Yeah, I did. He ain't scared boss. He don't want nothing to happen to the girl and the kid. But I'm thinking he ain't gonna be pushed too hard. He says he'll die for his country. He wants you to be at the next meeting."

"I am not paying you to think, Wilhelm. I will run the next meeting and Devin will come to heel or die."

"I'll make him talk, boss," Dieter says.

"He ain't scared a' you," Willi interjects. "You needle him any more and he's liable to kick your teeth in."

Dieter stands to throw his hat down by the side of his chair. "I'll rip that punk up. Ain't you or nobody else can stop me!"

Seidel speaks in a low voice, "Sit down, Dieter."

"I'll sit when I'm damn good and ready. You and Willi think you're so smart. You guys ain't runnin' me. I got a big part in this operation. I could blow this all wide open!"

In a louder voice Seidel barks, "Sit down, Dieter."

Dieter, fists clenched, advances on the table. Three shots ring out.

Dieter swallows hard, looking down into the still-smoking bore of Seidel's Luger. He backs up, hands behind him feeling for the chair.

Seidel flicks a spent cartridge case off the table. "I do wonder at times why I tolerate such stupid behavior. You will do exactly as I say or I will cut your heart out. I summoned you both here to make sure there will be no more slip ups. Wilhelm, I will not accept failure. We will, at any cost, obtain the radar information from Devin.

"I want to make sure our next meeting with Chief Devin is fruitful. You will bring him to me at an address I will give to you in Berkeley. You will put him in the back of the truck, blindfolded and handcuffed; then you will drive over the Bay Bridge. You will make sure no one can follow you.

"Do not forget I have given both of you new lives. Your new identities keep you out of the war and out of the clutches of your police. You have money and ration books. I can take all of that away should you fail to get me the radar information.

"Dieter, stay away from the sailor for now; you can dispose of him when we're done. Wilhelm, you will see to it that Devin understands he will bring what I want next Saturday. You both may go."

Willi and Dieter hurry toward the door. Willi has his hand on the door knob when Seidel calls out.

"Dieter, take your hat with you."

Dieter goes back to pick up his hat. He snatches it off the floor and pulls it down on his head, turning back to the door. Willi sheepishly looks at Seidel, then smirks pointing at Dieter's head. Dieter yanks the hat off to see three bullet holes stitched through the top of the cotton fabric.

Chapter 14

The following day in radar class Nick's swollen lip becomes the source of some ribald comments from his classmates. When Captain Shaver sees the damage to Nick's face he angrily quizzes him. Nick is trapped again; he can't tell Shaver without Keys' permission. Shaver storms off, leaving Nick with a growing anxiety. He feels angry and frustrated, wishing he had not gotten himself into such a mess.

After dinner that night Nick is surprised to see Agent Keys. Keys shows up at the barracks and asks Nick to take a walk with him.

"Your captain is plenty steamed. I wish I hadn't given him my phone number. So tell me all about it."

"They kept the boy somewhere," Nick says, "and I don't think they're gonna let him go. I don't think they're gonna let any of us go after they get what they want. I'm hoping you guys can stop 'em before it gets that far. You know those guys aren't gonna leave any witnesses behind, don't you? People here are talking about a lady that drove a bus for the shipyard that the cops just found murdered. I'm kinda wondering if her murder isn't part of this."

"I can tell you you're off on that one Nick. The bus lady's murder was a sex thing. The San Francisco cops got a line on the guy that did it. I'm glad it wasn't on my watch; I hate that stuff. I hate the sick bastards that do it. There isn't a punishment bad enough for those guys. Anyway let's get off that and tell me what happened in Crockett."

Nick recounts his Crockett story as they walk down Walnut Avenue, ending with his threat to do damage to the two henchmen.

"You're gonna have to hold your fire a little longer," Keys says. Naval officers walking by keep Nick busy with the required recognitions. "Look I'm gettin' dizzy with all this saluting. Have you got your pass to get off the base?"

Nick shows Keys his pass. "Okay, let's take my car and head over to Vallejo. We need a place to talk where I don't have to worry about being overheard."

Crossing over the G street causeway, Keys drives through Vallejo on Tennessee Street up into the hills above the city. Both men keep their thoughts to themselves until Keys parks his car on the top of a hill. They have a panoramic view overlooking the lights of Vallejo, Mare Island, and San Pablo Bay.

Keys reaches under the dash to pull back the handbrake lever. The metal handle makes a clacking noise as the spring-loaded catch rakes over serrated teeth to engage the brake. He settles back in the seat and pushes up the brim of his hat.

"Nick I don't want you gettin' hurt, but I don't want you to sour the deal by goin' off on Smith's boys. I want you to understand the importance of all this. We have top priority on this right now. I just took the doctored schematic to the radar department at Mare, and I've got a copy for you. We need to put this over on

Smith and his group, and try to find his contacts to German intelligence.

"I'm tellin' you this because Washington is pushing to close down on military information being passed to Japan and Germany. We just caught Velvalee Dickinson, the one they call the doll lady, in New York passing information to Japan.

"She never had a spy ring; she just asked the locals what was happening. She and her husband travelled to Seattle, Portland, and here to San Francisco. They'd watch the shipyards and strike up conversations. They found out what ships were being repaired and where they were going when they left port. That's all it takes. Practically anyone can sit up here and watch ships being built or repaired at Mare and pass that dope on. That house in Crockett you went to is a dandy place to watch naval traffic too. We have to stop that dope from gettin' out.

"I don't know if you've followed the newspaper stories about our Russkie friends, but I can tell you our big boss is fit to be tied. Headquarters just broke the news that they found a letter proving that our so-called allies, the Russians, have a major spy network in America. Their diplomats are running agents and sending out information in diplomatic pouches we can't touch.

"My point here is that everyone wants our dope, so if you and I can shut down an information gateway to Germany, that's a major source dried up. We'll learn from that and go for the next group that threatens our technology.

"I've had a detail of my men following Smith's boys and Smith. His two guys are easy to tail. Smith is cleverer and far more careful about being followed. We haven't been able to find his method of getting information out to his German masters.

"What's got me puzzled is that my men have reported that Smith's two boys are now being followed by another guy we don't know. Who or what the guy is after is anybody's guess at this point. You need to be aware there's a new fox in the henhouse. I'll let you know what we find out about the new guy.

Keys reaches behind the seat to get a weathered leather briefcase.

"Here's the doctored radar schematic. I know it's tough but I need more time to find Smith's contact."

Keys switches on the car's interior light. "Take your time, just memorize some portion of it. You can't keep the thing, I have to take it back with me when you've finished. You can show Smith how complicated it is to make each section of the drawing and tell him you can only memorize so much at a time."

Nick spreads out the drawing, studying the lines and symbols of the schematic, his finger tracing lines along the paper.

Keys cranks down his window to let out cigarette smoke. The cool night air fills the car. Fog rolls up over the western hills, pushed by Pacific Ocean wind currents. Rolling over the hill then down its slopes, the fog smothers the valleys; it creeps toward them consuming the landscape. The agent smokes his cigarette, his head moving in a constant vigil to survey their position.

Nick puts down the paper to light a cigarette. "I've got the gist of this, but I really need to set the paper down on a hard surface to trace the lines from one connection to another. I'll have to be able to ascertain how it works in order to explain it to Smith."

Keys crushes out his cigarette before flipping it out the window. "I'm glad you've got some idea of what that drawing means; it's all Greek to me. Just get what you can for now. I told your captain that I'd try to keep you on the shipyard during the week. I hope we can feed this to Smith on weekends when you would normally have liberty. Have you got enough right now to meet Smith?"

Nick strokes his chin in thought. "Give me a few more minutes to absorb this and I'm pretty sure I can draw the first quarter from memory."

After flipping out the cigarette butt Nick folds up the schematic and hands it to Keys. The agent starts the car, pushes the clutch in and pulls the shift lever down to crunch into first gear. "Call me when you know where the meet is. When you're done with Smith I'll be at the Rincon Hill place. You can meet me there and study the schematic for as long as you need."

The guard at Mare Island grudgingly lets them through after demanding to see Nick's pass, Keys' badge, and an explanation of their business on the shipyard.

"That boy's a bit too full of himself," Keys complains.

From the ghostly glare of the fog-laden causeway bridge's lights Nick can see Keys' frown. "Well, he doesn't have to worry about our rank and he's probably tired of standing out in the wet and cold."

Nick falls out at reveille the next morning, going about his duties until lunch when guilt forces him to check in with Doris.

She sits behind her typewriter cheerlessly hammering the keys. Her heavy makeup does not completely hide the blue-black bruising high on her cheek. Nick taps on the counter top.

Doris fingers down the top of the paper in the typewriter to see Nick. Her cheerless greeting is, "Oh hi, I have something for you."

Nick, curious by what caused the change in her demeanor, asks, "What's wrong Doris? Are you okay?"

Without a word Doris pushes back her chair to stand, then comes around the counter and motions Nick to follow her. They return to the same upstairs room as before. Doris turns to face Nick, taking a note paper from the pocket of her shirt.

Holding out the note she says, "Here, this is for you."

Nick takes the note, briefly examining it before returning his attention to Doris. She looks back at him with a defiant hands-on-hips stance.

"Why are you delivering this?" Nick asks.

"Because I have to do as those men say," Doris spits back. "They have taken over my house. If I ever want to see Benny again I have to obey them."

"I'm sorry, Doris. I'll make 'em leave you alone. We'll find a way to get Benny back if I have to beat those guys into the ground."

"I don't want you to beat up anyone. I just want Benny back."

"We can talk about what to do, Doris. I'm sorry I've been so preoccupied, but we can talk now."

"I don't want to talk anymore, Nick. I wasn't good enough for you before this, and now I don't care. I don't want any more men in my life. I'm tired of being a punching bag every time my husband gets drunk, or when some guy thinks he's tough. All I want from you is for you to do what they tell you to do so I can get Benny back.

"When Benny is back with me I'm leaving here. You can go play war with your buddies and I can make a life for Benny and me far away from all this shit. Don't look so shocked, sailor boy. Don't your shipmates talk like that all the time?"

"I'm, ah, really sorry, Doris. I didn't know."

Doris stops pacing the room. She comes face to face with Nick, then lashes out to smack his face.

"You didn't know, you didn't know. You didn't care that's what you didn't."

She swings her arm up but Nick deflects the blow, then grabs her arm.

Doris pushes her face up to Nick's. "Are you gonna hit me now? You wanta beat me up too?"

Nick lets go of her arm.

"I don't want to hurt you, Doris. I'm sorry you're so upset."

"I know you're sorry. All you men are sorry. You just be at the rail yard Saturday and give those bastards whatever they want. I don't care what you have to do, just get my son back. Now go, get out of here."

Chapter 15

Nick stands on the deck of the Vallejo ferry, relishing the cool salt spray and the ferry's rolling motion through the choppy bay. He longs for the day when he can get back to sea in his new sub.

His life on the sub in a war patrol is simple. Nick knows the job, he knows what is expected from him, and knows he excels. Life on the sub is kill or be killed, but there is that rush of adrenalin, that sense of purpose. He rues the day he met Doris and the days following when he listened to the woman's sad stories. Only Keys' words seemed to make some sense now.

After the confrontation with Doris, Nick called Keys to give him the instructions for his meet with Smith. Nick's mood quickly burst into an angry tirade. Bent over his desk Keys rubs his brow with his right hand; the phone clutched in his left hand is pressed hard against his ear.

"I get it Nick; you're pissed off. I probably would be too. You might wanta think of how Doris feels about her problems. The fact of the matter is that you're the man we need to do this job. Just think if Smith found someone else. Our radar secrets and who knows what else could have been stolen without us knowing it.

You, and the men on your sub, could be directly affected, as in sunk.

"If you hadn't come forward we wouldn't be pluggin' this leak. So buck up, go see Smith, sell him on the radar stuff. I'll work on my end as hard as I can to get this thing resolved. Make sure you get only a one-day pass. I don't want Smith to be able to hold on to you. Meet me at the hotel when you're free. You're the man I'm dependin' on, Nick. You're the best man I could hope for to get this dirty deal done."

Keys swivels in his chair rubbing his ear. "Okay, Jerry, get a coupla guys and two cars. I want you to tail Devin when Smith or his men pick him up. I gotta run this schematic over to Navy HQ and get a copy made for us.

"Nick says the pickup is at ten a.m. Saturday at the rail yard behind the piers. Be on the lookout for that other bird too. If Smith picks up Devin be watching for something cute, the guy's pretty clever. I want reports but don't use the car radios. You can phone me; if I'm not here, the switchboard will know where I am.

"If they use a car get the tag number, make, and model. I'll run it through the DMV. Don't let Smith sniff you out. If you can observe the meet go ahead, but I don't want Devin hurt. I don't want them to tumble to you either if they play nice. If there's any gun play I want Smith arrested not killed, okay?"

"Sure thing, Barry, I'll do my best."

The ferry bumps the pier's dock and Nick joins the rush off the landing. The crowd thins out at the Ferry Building. Nick crosses the busy Embarcadero to the dusty rail yard. There is no sign of anyone waiting for him there. He continues across the yard to Beach Street where he sees an old Ford bread van at the curb. One of Smith's henchmen slouches on the front fender smoking a cigarette.

The man flips the cigarette out in a long arc that sends sparks flying as it hits the street. He motions Nick toward the back of the van. There are no words exchanged as Nick gets in the van. The doors slam shut behind him. The only light in the back of the van comes from a small roof vent. There is a solid bulkhead dividing the driver's compartment from the back, and no windows in the rear doors. The compartment stinks of fish.

Nick scrambles to find a seat on a wooden crate as he hears the driver scrape into first gear before the van lurches forward from the curb. The ride starts out smooth; after going over what he assumes to be the Bay Bridge the driver begins weaving enough to throw Nick around on the metal flooring.

Finally wedging himself into a corner, he rides out the rest of the trip. After a sharp turn and bumping up an incline, all goes dark inside the van. Nick's head thumps an interior panel as the van stops. The van backs up slowly, the engine stops, and he can hear some kind of machinery start up. Nick's arms fly out searching for a hold when the van drops for what seems minutes before it stops abruptly, jouncing on its springs.

The rear doors of the van open to a dark background. A flashlight's circle of light marks the ground at the van's bumper. Nick hears Willi's voice, "The boss is waiting for you." The light swings to a door twenty feet to Nick's right.

Nick opens the door, taking a moment to let his eyes adjust to the light. The two henchmen push past him. The room is almost colorless. Three walls are pale rough-hewn wood; the fourth is cinder block with a large blackboard mounted on it. A bare, smooth concrete floor adds no color to the room.

Smith sits in an upholstered chair near the blackboard. His elbows rest on the arms of the chair, the fingers of his hands steepled. "I trust you have what I want, Devin. I will not tolerate further delay from you."

"Where's the boy?" Nick asks.

"You are not here to ask questions. If you do not have the radar plans I want you will not see the light of day again. Deliver, Devin," Smith growls, his fingers balling into fists.

"I can draw the first portion; I presume that's what the blackboard's for."

"Give me the key, Devin. Why is this radar unit important?"

Nick moves to the blackboard. "Will you understand anything I draw or tell you about it?"

Smith rises from the chair. "I will not warn you again about asking questions. Give me the key information."

"Alright, keep your shirt on. I suppose the phrase you're looking for is centimetric, the new radar is centimetric."

Smith sits down and crosses his legs. "That will do for a start. How is this made possible?"

Nick looks down at Smith wondering how much he knows. "The Brits have invented the cavity magnetron that generates frequencies that can operate between 3 and 30 megahertz."

Smith grins up at Nick. "And what do you Americans call these frequencies?"

"We call them microwaves."

Smith sinks back in the chair with his elbows on the arms to steeple his fingers again. "Yes, yes, now we begin. Draw the schematic for me, all of it."

Nick picks a stick of chalk from the bottom ledge of the chalkboard. "I can draw the first part that I've memorized. The rest will come in two more parts. I can't memorize more than that and be able to make an accurate drawing. I told you that in the beginning."

Smith waves his hand at the blackboard. "Start drawing. I will determine how we go from there."

Nick spends the next forty-five minutes drawing. He stands back inspecting the schematic, erases a line, then redraws the line adding a resistance value. "That's all I've got. You know the duplexers are extremely complex. I need to study that part of the Mare Island schematic to get it right. If I don't get it the pulse receiver won't work. Do you understand?"

Smith stands behind Nick inspecting the blackboard. "Yes, it is complex, any fool knows that, Devin. I thought you might have trouble with the duplexers. You have two more chances, no more. My men will pick you up at the same place next Saturday."

"What about the boy?" Nick asks.

Smith slaps the back of Nick's head. "I told you no more questions. The boy remains with us until you have finished. Willi, take Devin back to San Francisco."

At the door Willi tells Nick to turn around and walk backwards out of the room. Dieter pulls the door closed, putting the three men in total darkness. Willi flicks his flashlight to life and directs Nick to the back of the van. Nick climbs in heading for the corner to wedge himself in on the now familiar crate. He hears the machinery start and feels the van elevate.

They return to the rail yard where the van stops and Willi opens the rear doors. Nick steps out, squinting in the bright sunshine. Willi drives away without a word. Walking with his hands in his pockets, deep in thought, Nick becomes conscious of his location on Grant Avenue in North Beach. Walking another block Nick ducks into an Owl Drug Store to use the phone booth.

Nick drops a nickel into the slot and dials FBI headquarters. The switchboard operator puts him through to Barry Keys.

"Barry, I'm back in San Francisco. I can't tell you much about where we met because they kept me in the back of an old bread van with no windows. I ducked into an Owl Drug Store to call because I think I'm being followed. Do you have someone on me?"

Keys at his desk says, "No, Nick, I don't have anyone covering you right now. I got a report from Jerry an hour ago. He followed your van to a warehouse in Berkeley. A man was seen coming from the outside of that building carrying a canvas bag shortly before your van came out. Jerry's pretty sure it was the same man he spotted when he was tailing Smith's guys.

"He sent one of the teams covering you to follow the bag guy and Jerry followed your van back to the rail yard. He's still on the bread van now. Hold on Nick, I've got team two on another line." Keys comes back on Nick's line moments later.

"Nick, team two followed the bag guy back across the bridge and lost him in heavy traffic on The

Embarcadero. That puts him in your general area. Have you spotted the guy following you?"

"No, it's more of a feeling than anything. I did the window reflection trick you taught me, but I couldn't see anyone that stood out."

"That's okay, Nick. The guy's good, we know that. Tell you what, go to the fountain and have something to eat. Stay there for a half-hour, that'll give me time to get to the Rincon Hill place. When you finish eating go straight to the hotel; don't look for the guy following you. I'll station my men outside the hotel and we'll have the guy.

"I'm itchin' to find out how many players we've got in this deal. See you at the hotel. Just be cool, Nick."

Chapter 16

Nick's cab driver drones on with his graphic views of jungle warfare. The old man has never been out of America but knows the right way the Marines should fight the Japanese in the Solomon Islands. Nick stays calm, not looking about for the man who could be following, and only hears snippets before the cab pulls up to the curb in front of the Rincon Hill hotel.

At the room Barry Keys hands Nick an Acme beer. "Thought we'd try a local brand while we wait to see if we have us a visitor."

Nick takes a sip and grins. "Well it's cold, thanks."

Keys puts his beer down to light a cigarette. "So tell me about Smith. Did you sell him?"

"He's hooked okay. I was concerned because he did know centimetric and that we call those frequencies microwaves. I fed him a line about duplexers and pulse receivers that he didn't get. So he's not really hep to the whole concept but he does know the key words."

"Amil Seidel is the man's real name," Keys says. "He's been a failed actor and cheap gigolo; he had nothing until the war started. Now he's a big property owner. That warehouse in Berkeley they took you to is just one of the places he's got on both sides of the bay.

The guys that picked you up are a local couple a 4-Fers. They've both got long histories of petty crimes."

"Yeah they wear that like a stink. A coupla bully boys that can't fight. There's not a service that'd want 'em," Nick snaps. "Hey, how's the guy who's following me gonna know what room we're in?"

Before closing the curtains, Keys switches on the lights. "The man at the desk's clued in. He'll send the guy here. I've got two men posted outside. Relax, we may be in for a long wait. I take it you didn't have any trouble with Smith's two meatballs."

"No trouble. I slid around like a pinball in the back of that old van until I wedged myself in a corner. There was hardly any light and it smelled like dead fish."

"I thought that was just your seamen's scent," Keys quips.

"Ha, ha, a little Old Spice on you'd go a long way."

Keys lifts his arm to sniff at his arm pit. "Oh, a cut so deep, and to think I was just havin' nothing but fun."

"Okay, I'm sorry, that was outta line," Nick sheepishly replies.

Keys doubles over laughing. "Geez man, if that was the worst thing someone said to me I'd be happy. I'm just tryin' ta lighten the mood."

The silly banter is interrupted by a knocking at the door.

"Probably one of my guys wantin' to know when they can knock off for the night."

Nick's eyes go wide as he watches Keys back away from the opened door with his hands raised. Over the FBI man's shoulder he sees a big grey-haired man with a pistol aimed at Keys' chest. The man has a lumpy canvas bag hanging from a strap over his shoulder. Without turning completely around he kicks the door closed.

"Get back with your friend," the pistol-waver barks. "Both of you back up to the wall with your hands up. I want the radar schematic."

"I don't have any such thing," Keys replies.

"I know you have it, Keys, I know everything. Turn around and face the wall. I'll take a look in your briefcase. Keep your hands up!"

Nick and Keys turn toward the rear wall. Nick slowly raises his hands then slaps the light switch off. As the room goes dark he pushes Keys hard to his left and darts to his right. The pistol reports are deafening, muzzle flashes light up the room. There is a kaleidoscope effect as Keys returns fire. The big man grunts, a moment later light from the hall bursts into the room and silhouettes the man as he runs out.

Nick runs toward the door. Keys yells, "Stop! Don't go out the door!"

Devin pauses, then peeks out into the hall way. Two more shots ring out splintering the door frame. Nick stumbles back almost losing his balance. Keys crouches at the door and fires his pistol up the hallway.

Both Keys and Nick hear the big man's foot falls pound down the hallway. Barry yanks a speed loader from his pocket, dumps the spent cartridges, reloads the revolver, then runs after the big man. Nick is quickly at the FBI man's heels and tries to pass him. Keys thrusts out his arm to block Nick. "Stay behind me, I've got the gun."

They both bolt to the end of the hallway, up the stairs, and out onto the roof. The lights of the city cast odd shadows on the roof of the building. The black tarpaper roof in those shadows makes it seem like stepping off into a pool of bottomless space. Nick grabs Keys' shoulder, motioning to a roof vent. "The guy ducked behind that vent," Nick whispers.

Keys pushes Nick away and snaps off a shot at the vent. The big man fires off two rounds, one finding Keys' left leg, knocking him down. The second round locks the slide back on the big man's automatic, the magazine empty. Nick runs around the left side of the vent to grab at the man.

The big man pulls away; Nick snags the canvas bag. As they both tug at the bag Nick can see wet blood on the man's shirt. He jerks hard on the strap several times before the big man grunts and lets go, sending Nick to the ground clutching the bag.

Nick scrambles to his feet, drops the bag, and runs after the man. They both head for the edge of the roof. In the existing light the roof of the adjacent building looks to be an easy jump. The big man takes long strides before looking back to see Nick closing on him.

The shadows hide the dark roof's ledge. When the big man is almost on top of the ledge he tries to readjust his stride. He pulls his leg up having misjudged the ledge's height; his shin crashes into the ledge sending him headfirst across the narrow space into the side of the adjacent building.

Nick sees the man stumble at the roof's edge. He stands transfixed as the man, arms flailing the air, goes over the ledge. The dull thump of the man's head crashing into the brickwork of the opposite building, followed by the sound of the body striking the pavement below are sounds that Nick will carry for some time. Looking over the ledge he sees the big man's broken body lying in a pool of blood.

Running back to Agent Keys, Nick finds him pulling his belt tight around his thigh.

"Are you okay, Barry?"

"I think so; the bullet went right through my leg right above my knee. I don't think it got any bone, but the hole's bleeding like a stuck pig. I saw the guy go over the edge. I take it he didn't sprout wings and fly away."

"He won't be doing any more flying. Let's get you to a hospital. Hey, where the hell are your guys anyway?"

"They must be on siesta, but they're gonna be on busted asses when I see 'em again. You got the guy's canvas bag, didn't you? I could just see him goin' over. I didn't see he had the bag."

"Lie back down. I'll get the bag and call for the medics. Don't be dumb, Barry, lie back; you don't wanta bleed out and ruin my medal for savin' your hide."

"You, savin' my hide, that'll be the damned day."

Nick finds the canvas bag; he goes back the ledge to pick up the pistol the big man dropped, shoves it into the bag, then rushes back to the fallen FBI man whose eyes are closed.

"Barry, come on Barry, open up man."

Nick feels for Keys' pulse and gets a weak throbbing. He remembers to release the belt tourniquet briefly, then runs across the roof and down the stairs.

Chapter 17

Bounding down the stairs he almost knocks over Jerry Walsh, Keys' partner.

"What's going on, Devin; where's Keys?"

"He's on the roof, shot in the leg, and needs to get to the hospital. Where the hell have you guys been?"

Walsh pushes by Nick to run up the stairs. Nick turns to follow.

Walsh is bent over Keys, his finger on the prone agent's throat. He turns to Nick who is standing to the side.

"Gimme a hand hoisting him over my shoulder. We need to get outta here before the cops show up. Gimme his gun."

Walsh takes Keys' gun that Nick picked up and puts it in his pocket. He shifts Keys' dead weight on his shoulder and heads for the stairs.

Walsh calls to Nick over his shoulder, "Shut the door behind you and wipe the knob. Get everything outta the room, wipe it down too. I'll meet you out back."

At the room, Nick grabs Keys' briefcase. He throws the beer cans and trash in a pillowcase, looks around the rooms for anything else before wiping everything he could remember he or Keys touched. He tries to yank the door shut, but has to take time to clear splinters from the door frame to get it to close.

On his way downstairs Nick wonders why no one on his floor seems to be curious. Walsh has the engine running at the mouth of the alley when Nick arrives. He has Keys laid out on the rear seat of the Chevy four-door.

"Come on, Devin; the cops are gonna be here any second."

Nick throws the briefcase and pillowcase in as Walsh pulls out of the alley to head north. He clambers into the front seat, just getting the door shut as an SFPD cop car roars toward them, red lights flashing, siren blasting.

Walsh goes left on Bush, then right on Van Ness to Lombard. He drives hard, weaving through traffic keeping an eye out for any police. The Chevy's six-cylinder engine pulls them uphill onto the Golden Gate Bridge.

"Where are you going?" Nick asks.

Walsh replies keeping his eyes on the road, "I know a vet in Sausalito."

"A vet! Keys needs a hospital, man."

"Look, Devin, I'm runnin' the show now. If Keys was conscious he'd be doin' the same thing. When the cops see all that blood on the roof and in the alley they're gonna be checkin' the hospitals. If we take Keys to any hospital around here they might find him and that could led 'em to you. If they get on to you we've lost the whole ball game."

Nick looks over at Walsh, who remains concentrated on the road. "What are the cops going to think about the man in the alley?"

"The man in the alley is in a body bag in the trunk. I gotta get his finger prints before he can sleep with the fish."

Down the hill on the north side of the Waldo Tunnel Walsh turns right and heads into Sausalito. The little city has tripled in size since Bechtel's Marinship started cranking out Liberty ships. Bright lights of the shipyard radiate a sphere of light in the sky north of the city where thousands of men and women from all over the United States are working around the clock for the war effort.

Walsh snakes around the narrow twisting streets. The Chevy's headlights cast their beams crazily back and forth before resting on a small placard on a fence lettered Dr. Ross Valentino Veterinary Physician. The small house perched on a hillside is dark in the still night.

"Stay in the car, Devin, the Doc spooks easy. I'll have to talk him into this."

Walsh goes to the door to push the doorbell. He pushes the button several times before disappearing around the back of the house. Nick turns to see how Keys is doing. In the dim light he sees Keys' forehead glistening with sweat. A light comes on at the front door. A dark-haired man pulling on a robe comes through the door with Walsh behind him.

"I don't like this, Walsh," the man whispers.

"Look lover boy, you owe me. I could still run you in for takin' that girl across the state line."

Valentino gestures to Walsh with his hands to keep his voice down. "Okay, okay. Get him inside, just be quiet about it."

Agent Walsh lowers his voice, "Turn that porch light out, Doc, and we'll bring him in."

Nick and Walsh each get a hand under Keys' arms to pull him from the car. As the two men lift the wounded agent Keys' eyes snap open.

"What's goin' on? Where am I?"

Nick helps Keys to his feet to lean against the car. "You don't remember getting' shot?" Nick asks.

Keys looks down at his leg. "Aw shit, look at my pants, I just got these from Sears."

Walsh laughs. "You silly bastard, whata ya think your leg looks like? Come on, Barry, let's get you into the Doc's house."

Valentino dries his hands on a towel in his operating room. "Put him up on the table."

Walsh helps Keys onto the table. Nick grabs a phone book to put under Keys' head.

Valentino uses a pair of scissors to cut through the cuff of Keys' pants. He rips the pant leg above the wound throwing the bloodied material over Keys' other leg.

"Aw shit," Keys moans.

The veterinarian wipes down the wound with an alcohol-soaked cloth, making Keys flinch.

Pulling an overhead light over the vet says, "Hold still, agent, this could be serious."

Valentino inspects the wound carefully. He wipes the blood away again and with both hands gently opens the wound on the front of Keys' leg.

"Help me turn him over; I want to look at the exit wound."

Keys is surprisingly docile when Nick and Walsh help him to turn on his stomach.

The doctor holds on to Keys' leg as he wipes the exit wound. The vet pulls the light down to inspect the wound, then reaches into a drawer to get a pair of tweezers. Holding the wound open with his thumb and forefinger, he probes the wound with the tweezers. Valentino holds the tweezers up to the light.

"I've got a bone fragment here; you better get this man to a hospital. He needs a facility where they can amputate the leg should that be necessary. If a small bone fragment gets into his blood stream it could kill him."

Keys turns over with surprising speed. "Doc, sew me up right now. Nobody's gonna saw off my leg."

"I can't take that responsibility, agent."

Keys reaches inside coat, then pats his pockets. "Where the hell's my gun? Walsh, tell this guy to sew me up or shoot 'em. I've had worse than this, man. Now, goddamnit man," Keys points to his leg, "get to it."

Nick watches the vet's hands shake as he tries to thread the needle.

Keys lies across the back seat of Walsh's car, his head above the seat back. "We need to get Nick back to the ferry. Nick, call me Monday, we'll go over the plan for your next meet."

Nick turns in the car's front seat to answer Keys. "Are you gonna be working?"

"Sure thing. I've had worse fallin' off a bicycle.

Nick laughs. "Red Rider G-man, one tough hombre."

"You betcha," Keys snorts.

Walsh pulls up to the ferry terminal. Nick gets out of the car, crosses around the front of the car when

Keys calls out to him. "Hey Nick, thanks man, I owe you one."

"You betcha," Nick says, saluting back at the car.

"Gimme a ride back to my place, Jerry, will ya?"

Chapter 18

Keys' apartment is off Mason Street a few blocks down from Union Square. Walsh looks up at the rear view mirror at Keys in the back seat. "Wake up, Barry, we're here. Uh, Mary isn't back, is she?"

Keys rubs his eyes, then lifts himself up on the seat. "No such luck. But then she left because she couldn't stand me comin' home banged up at all hours. So at least she won't be cryin' her eyes out this time. Gimme a hand gettin' out, will ya?"

Keys' corner apartment is on the third floor. The bay window's curtains are open to the city lights below. Keys hobbles in to switch on the lights, then pulls the drapes closed. "I need a drink, Jerry. How 'bout pourin' a couple? There's a bottle a scotch in the cabinet above the ice box."

"You sure you can drink scotch after those pills the Doc gave you?"

"I'm fine, Jerry. That stuff is good, but I want to go over the events I missed while I was out. A drink ain't gonna kill me."

Walsh notes that the kitchen is just as neat as when Keys' wife was keeping house. He had some concern when he found out that his long time partner and friend's wife had left him. The clean, neat apartment tells Walsh that Keys has not let himself or the place go. He finds the scotch and glasses and pours two, neat.

Keys knocks back half the drink and settles back in his chair. "I've got a lot of questions, Jerry. We've gotta get on top of this quick. Pour me another splash, will ya?"

Keys, arms folded peacefully across his chest, is snoring lightly when Walsh returns from the kitchen. Walsh rinses the glasses in the sink then drapes a blanket over Keys before slipping out of the apartment.

The next morning across town the phone on Walsh's night stand clamors relentlessly. Walsh rolls over trying to focus on the clock's hands. "Yeah, talk. Keys, what the hell are you doin' up? So it's 9 a.m., it's Sunday man, go back to bed, I need my beauty sleep."

Back on Mason Street, Keys puts the grocery bags down to get the door of his apartment unlocked. After putting the groceries away he picks up his phone to dial. "Okay Walsh, it's 11 o'clock, get your dead ass over here. I just got fresh chorizo, jalapenos, and onions. My wake-up omelet's gonna be ready in twenty minutes; saddle up, pilgrim."

Walsh showers and shaves, then goes out the front door of his place to be greeted with a wet fog covering the city. He moans, cursing the weather, before getting into his car. The vacuum wipers slap the windshield ,then slow as the car climbs up Mason Street hill.

Keys answers the door wearing an apron.

"God, that smells good, Keys. Is it lethal?"

"It'll put a fire in your belly, that's for sure. Pull up a pew."

Walsh takes a drink of water to cool his mouth after mopping up his plate with a flour tortilla. Keys opens two beer cans and places one on the table in front of Walsh.

Keys gathers up the plates then sits down at the table. Taking a pull from his beer he asks, "Okay, first question: what the hell happened? Why didn't the second team tell me the guy was coming up to the room? They were supposed to call me when they spotted him."

"Dick took Denny to the hospital, looks like appendicitis. He called me through dispatch on his way there. I got to the hotel and went in to ask the desk clerk if the guy had showed. I heard gun shots and ran up the stairs. Devin was comin' down. We went back up and I put you over my shoulder to get you in the car. Devin went back to clean up the room."

"Dammit, did the cops get the big guy? I saw him go off the roof."

"Take it easy, Barry. I got the guy in the trunk of the car before we took you to the vet. After I left you sleeping last night I got his finger prints and his wallet. I drove down past Half Moon Bay, got the body out of the car, stripped it and noted two old scars: one on his left arm, one on his left leg. You got him under his right arm, musta busted a coupla ribs.

"I waded out as far as I could and sent him off. With any luck he's either shark bait or on the way to Australia. I got home about two minutes before you called the first time. At least it felt like that. The bag he carried's got a recorder in it. The thing's pretty small. There's a notebook and a codebook and some other stuff. I'm gonna go to the shop and see if I can find if we've got anything on the guy."

"Good work, Jerry, I'll grab my coat and go with you."

"You sure you're up to it?"

"Hell, those pills your vet gave me could make an elephant dance. Let's go."

Keys and Walsh walk into the stately 111 Sutter Street Hunter-Dulin Building. Keys takes a moment, waiting for the elevator, to take in the richness of the lobby. He often marvels at the beautiful gold and jade trimmed murals on the walls and ceiling, the inlaid marble floor, a very fancy place for the FBI, he muses. The elevator's gold doors open and the two FBI men take a glass smooth ride up to the 17th floor. Room number 1729 houses the FBI offices.

Walsh goes to the files to see if they have anything on the identification he found in the big man's wallet. Keys heads to his desk with the canvas bag the big man was carrying. Pulling the recorder out, he sets it on the desk, then removes the rest of the contents from several pouches sewn into the interior of the bag. He notes with some interest the pistol the man shot him with is a well-used small caliber six-shot automatic.

Putting the bag on the floor next to the desk, he arranges the codebook, notepad, wallet, and other items neatly on the desktop around the recorder. The recorder is much smaller than anything he has seen before. It has a metal case Keys opens to find two magnetic wire reels, a battery compartment and buttons to record and play back on the ends of the case.

Keys turns the recorder over, feeling its weight. On the back is an emblem stamped "made in Germany". One side of the case has a round hole marked "mike". The agent picks up one of the three microphones on the desk. It is two inches in diameter and a half inch thick; the cord on this microphone is two feet long. Another two microphones have cords wound on spools that look many feet long.

A device that looks like a doctor's stethoscope has the same plug on the end of its cord that the microphones have. Keys works the lever on the top of the box marked "on-off". The magnetic tape spools spin. He switches the lever off, then pushes the rewind button and switches the lever back on. The spools spin in the opposite direction rewinding, then stop. He switches the lever off then back on and the spools begin to spin which should make the recording audible. There is no sound.

Keys plugs the stethoscope in and hears voices. His face changes from a curious frown to surprise; he hears a voice he does not recognize giving the date and time. A moment later, holding the earpieces tightly to his ears, he recognizes this voice: "Well it's cold, thanks," says Nick Devin. The first words Nick said at the Rincon Hill hotel room.

Walsh runs into the room waving sheets of paper. "We've got him. The guy's got a hell of a sheet."

Keys looks up at Walsh countering with, "He's been recording us at the Rincon Hill place!"

Walsh drops his arm holding the papers. "What? How the hell did he do that?"

"It's been killin' me, Jerry, tryin' to figure how the guy got on to us. I thought we must have a leak either here or the Navy guys. It has to be someone at the Rincon Hill place. The guy had to have access to the room and know when we'd be there. He said he knew I had the schematic."

"I thought maybe it was the kid," Walsh says.

"You mean Devin? No way; the kid's solid. I wouldn't call him a kid to his face either, man. He's a quick thinker; he shoved me out of the way just as he shut off the lights when our dead guy demanded the goods. I had to hold him back to keep him from gettin' shot. He was after the guy; right on his tail. If anything, we've put him in a bad place neither of us would like to be in."

Keys takes the sheets from Walsh. "So what have we got on the dead guy?"

"His name was Thomas Clark," Walsh explains. "We've got plenty on him, dating back to the longshoremen's strike in '34. He was a Communist Party member arrested with a gang that was turning over trucks by the train depot. Since then he's been arrested for assault, burglary, B&E, attempted murder, and murder for hire.

"In every case, witnesses never made it to trial. He's always had expensive lawyers, way above anything he could afford. The murders were on communist hit lists. So it's safe to say our boy Tommie was working for the Communist party. We know the Russian's are after the stuff at Berkeley, but maybe that's just the tip of the iceberg."

"Have we got a current address for Clark?" Keys asks.

Walsh takes the papers back from Keys. "Yeah, I saw it here on one of the sheets." Shuffling through the sheets Jerry finds the one with an address. "Yeah, here it is; I think he's in one of those shacks off Innes down by Hunters Point."

Keys puts Clark's gear back in the canvas bag. "Let's go; he's gotta have more recordings than this one. We may be able to bust this case wide open if we can find 'em."

Keys swings out the cylinder of his revolver to check the load. Satisfied, he adds, "We'll stop by the hotel on Rincon Hill on the way, and see if we can rid the place of rats."

Chapter 19

The two FBI men walk into the hotel, brushing rainwater from their coat sleeves. There is no one at the front counter. Keys draws his gun, holding it down by his side. He motions Walsh to the right side of the counter, then smacks the bell on the counter hard, several times.

A small man sporting a green plastic visor shuffles in from a room behind the counter.

"Can I help you?" he asks.

"Where's the guy that's usually on the counter?" Keys growls.

"Gone."

"Gone where?" Walsh demands.

The man starts at Walsh's voice, spinning his head toward the agent. Recovering his composure he looks back to Keys. "Who wants to know?"

Keys shifts his gun to his left hand and takes out his FBI identification. Holding the I.D. out Keys says, "This is FBI business. Who are you and where's Sammy, the guy that's usually here?"

"Oh, okay, I'm the guy that looks after the books. Sammy, the night manager, and the two elevator-lobby boys are gone. I don't have any idea where they went.

114

They got the cash from the till and took a powder. Outside of the maids, I'm the only one here."

Keys puts his I.D. and gun away. "Where's the owner, Dan Jefferies?"

The little man takes off the visor to wipe his brow on his sleeve. "Mr. Jefferies is down in L.A. I called him this morning when I came in to tell him that Sammy and his crew were gone with this week's money. He's plenty steamed."

Keys hands the man his card. "You know anything about Sammy and his crew?"

"The cops were here asking about gun shots; I heard that. The next thing I know is the place ain't got nobody to run it. Like I said, I just do the books. I didn't mingle with their crowd. This is a place where you're not supposed to know anybody. Mr. Jefferies told me to keep my nose in the books and not ask any questions."

Keys buttons his coat. "Okay, tell Jefferies when he gets back that I want to talk to him."

Keys gets in Walsh's car; they drive over to Third Street headed south. By the time they get to Evans Avenue the rain stops. As Evans becomes Hunters Point Boulevard the sun breaks through. Keys can see Alameda across the bay, where beams of sunlight bore holes in the clouds to highlight areas of the island.

Keys slips into a reverie; he loves the Bay Area. He has had a long career with the government, being shuffled to different parts of the country, moving every few years. More agents are coming to San Francisco now. The Bureau is growing but communications about other areas of investigation are becoming secretive.

Keys feels left out, adrift; he has been a senior officer here, always in the know.

The view reminds him of the happy days before the war, before he was shot in the chest. The World's Fair at Treasure Island where the lights and attractions dazzled him and his wife Mary. They walked hand in hand marveling at the sculptures and pavilions from countries they had only read about. Mary tugged him away from the crowds at Sally Rand's Nude Ranch exhibition saying she had a better dance in mind when they got home. San Francisco was their "City by the Bay".

The night Keys was shot he was following a criminal thought to be passing counterfeit twenty dollar bills. Another FBI agent had told Keys the man was a minor criminal but, in fact, he was the powerful leader of the counterfeit gang. Slipping around a building at the corner of Montgomery and Pine, Keys saw the man he was following meet two men in a car. Strong headlight beams pierced the night, splashing Keys' silhouette larger than life against the brick walls that had him hemmed in. He had nowhere to run. Brilliant flashes of gun fire, then a searing pain were the last things Keys remembered about that night.

Days later Walsh found Keys at City Hospital tagged as a John Doe. There was no identification found on him when he was brought in. Mary had been frantic, calling the FBI office, then begging Walsh to find out what happened to her husband. She said she knew something bad had happened, she could feel it.

Walsh checked hospitals in the city, then in adjacent counties, then morgues; no one had an FBI man. Walsh walked through scores of halls and wards before finding Keys. It was not until Keys heard Mary's voice that he came to and realized he had been shot.

The days before Walsh found Keys had traumatized Mary. She knew she could not stand it again. While he convalesced she begged Keys to quit. He said he couldn't; she said she couldn't stand to go through the grief again and left him.

Mary now lives in a housing unit at Marinship. She works in the drafting office and loves her job. Keys thinks of going private if the Bureau asks him to transfer again. He wants Mary back; she told him she would always love only him. If he were to quit the FBI maybe he could allay her fear of his being hurt or killed. He thinks of her more and more: he's got to get her back before some wartime desk jockey steals her heart.

Walsh snaps Keys from his daydreams. Turning off Innes Avenue Walsh says, "There's the shack."

The shack sits alone on a small rise. It is crudely built of rough-cut wood twenty yards from the water. Skeletal remnants of old small craft litter the ground surrounding the shack. Diesel fuel and various types of oil give a multicolored sheen to the water close to shore. This section of shoreline stinks of fuel oil and dead fish. A half mile down the road is the clamoring US Navy ship repair station, Hunters Point.

Keys grunts, pulling on the door frame getting out of the car. He and Walsh walk slowly up to the shack, their hands resting on the butts of their pistols. There is a padlock on the door facing them. Keys motions Walsh to circle the place. Walsh completes the walk around.

"There's no other door and one curtained window toward the water. I'll look around for something to spring the door."

"Don't bother," Keys says, "throw me the car keys and I'll get a tire iron."

Keys walks back from the car to see Walsh forcing a length of rebar under the padlocked hasp. Keys drops the tire iron. Ignoring the pain from his leg, he runs with a wobble trying to reach Walsh.

Chapter 20

Keys grabs at the collar of Walsh's coat; his fingers lock on the fabric giving enough purchase to yank as hard as he can. Both men fall back to the ground as the door flies open followed by a deafening boom. Shotgun pellets fly through the opening. They hear a series of pops then a whoosh sound; flames blast out from the door opening.

Winded, Walsh helps Keys get up off the ground. They both move back away from the heat. "Jesus, I guess you saved my bacon this time."

Keys massages his leg. "Yeah, well if we were keepin' score, you'd still be ahead."

"How'd you know the door was rigged?"

"I'll tell you later; call the Fire Department, will you? There's so much oil saturated in the ground here the fire could spread."

Keys and Walsh wait well back from the fire engine while the firemen pump water over the area. With the fire out firemen trample through the ruins soaking down any hot spots. The only thing recognizable in the rubble is a cast iron wood stove, a haze of heat and steam still shimmering from its surface.

Keys looks at Walsh shaking his head. "I doubt there's anything left to see. Let's have a look anyway before we head back."

Walsh uses the length of rebar to sift through the black muck while Keys circles the perimeter looking for evidence that might be buried.

"Find anything?" Keys asks.

"No, whatever was here burned up. There's only ash; it burned right down to the sand."

On the way back to Sutter Street Walsh asks Keys how he knew the place was rigged.

"The boss sent me up to Seattle to look into a guy the cops killed in the longshoreman's strike. Daffron, I think was the guy's name. The cops were riled because one of the sheriff's deputies was killed too. They were looking for anyone associated with the Communist Party. A few of the cops decided it was a perfect opportunity to wipe out the Reds.

"I followed four cops that were makin' a lot of noise. These guys were your garden variety pool hall bullies. They weren't looking for justice; they just wanted to hurt someone. They drove out of town to a dirt road in the woods. I had to hang back to keep from bein' spotted.

"The dust they kicked up from the road kept me on 'em. I see their car stopped in front of an old shack. By the time I get outta my car and find a spot to watch from, one of the bad boys heads to the shack's door with a crowbar. He shoves the bar in the door jam, busts the door in and almost falls into the place.

"A boom comes a split second later and the cop falls back outta the shack with a belly full a buckshot. Someone rigged the shack with a shotgun pointed at the door. When I saw you at the door of Clark's place that picture snapped into my head. I thought for a second how dumb I'd look yankin' you down if nothin' happened."

"I'm damned happy you didn't take a lotta time to make up your mind about it."

"Head for a Blum's, will ya, Jer? I'm hungry; we need a little something before we get to the shop. I'm anxious to hear those recordings Clark made but my belly's makin' growlin' noises."

Walsh finds a place off Market to park. "Why don't you wait here, Barry? I'll run in and get it. Whatta you want?"

Keys hands Walsh some dollar bills from his wallet. "Get me a tuna on rye and some fries. Buy us a can a Almondettes too."

Walsh gets out of the car, turns back toward the car when he hears Keys yell, "Make sure the can's got a key on it."

Walsh waves in acknowledgment crossing Market Street.

The two FBI men sit at Keys' desk at the Sutter Street field office eating the Blum's sandwiches.

Keys inspects the Almondettes can, then sets it back on his desk to dip his hands in the French fry bag.

Walsh wipes his mouth with a napkin to ask Keys about the Almondettes can. "So what's with the can, Barry? It's got the key on it."

"It's a long story, Jer."

"Well, I got time."

"It's kinda embarrassing. Stupid really."

Walsh grins, leaning in to share the secret. "If you can't tell me who you gonna tell?"

"Okay, I let myself in for it. I came back from a King City kidnap before the war. Mary was at her sister's; her sister was about to give birth. So I cross the bridge thinkin' of dinner. I go to Blum's to get a hamburger and fries to go; I see all those cans of candy on the way to the register. So I grab a can a Almondettes.

"I get in my car and think instead a goin' home I'll drive out to Crissy Field and watch the ships. It's an end a summer day and beautifully clear, no fog. The water's like a lake, I saw that from the bridge coming in. Anyway I drive off, find a place to park and take the bag to a bench.

"The burger's the best, the fries are crunchy like I like 'em. I finish and wipe the grease off thinking all the time about my dessert. I pull the can outta the bag and the key opener's gone. Ya know, I went a little nuts. I wanted that candy. I'm lookin at the can plenty pissed I can't get it open.

"With my pocket knife I get the tab bent and I'm tryin' to pull the metal strip. The metal slits my thumb, blood spurts and I'm gettin' mad. It's gettin' dark out and I'm havin' an insane thought a shootin' the top of the can off. I take my gun out, shake the rounds outta the cylinder and pinch the strip between the hammer and the frame.

"I'm pullin' on the strip; got it about half way round when I turn the can with my left hand to pull the strip on around. The metal edge that's open cuts my left hand's fingers and I drop the can. The can's on the ground, my gun's beside it and there's a kid that appears from nowhere. He's standin' there lookin' at me with these big googley eyes like I'm crazy.

122

"I shoo the kid away, pull out a napkin to wipe off the blood; the napkin's got salt on it from the fries. My gun's got blood on it, the can's got blood on it, and my hands sting like hell from the salt. I look at the whole mess and start laughin'. What an idiot. I'm just glad Mary wasn't there to witness that one."

Walsh is laughing so hard he can't get words out; cola streams from his nose.

"If you tell anybody I'll wring your neck."

Walsh wipes his face, still chuckling. "Are you kiddin'? You musta gotten that one outta a comic book. Man, that's better 'an Daffy Duck! You can spin a yarn, Barry, I'll give you that. I can just see the cover now."

Walsh puts up his hands as if displaying the comic book's cover. He moves his right hand like he is writing out the script.

"Agent X-10, locked in mortal combat with his most feared enemy. Disarmed and horribly wounded, our hero fights for his life. Who will win this titanic battle? The fate of the world hangs on the outcome. Good verses evil; Agent X-10 faces his most ferocious foe, the dreaded Cana Candy."

Two other agents enter the room to check in. They look at Keys and Walsh with some curiosity before waving a greeting.

Keys makes busy gathering up the food wrappers to throw in the trash. He takes out his notepad to flip through the pages. "Okay, Jer, see if you can run down the registration on the bread van. Devin said it smelled like fish inside, maybe that means something. I'll listen to the recordings we've got."

Walsh stands to deliver an elaborate salute. "Aye aye, Agent X-10."

123

Keys retrieves the canvas bag taking out the recorder and the pouch with the wire spools. Putting on the ear phones Keys plays the spools one by one, their full lengths. The tiny spools run for only a few minutes each. Making a few notes Keys tiredly rubs his face in his hands.

Walsh returns with his notepad. "All I can get on a Sunday is a name and address in El Centro on the bread van. I can chase it down more tomorrow when everybody gets back to work."

"Good enough, Jer. All that's on these spools is the meeting between Seidel and Devin, and me and Devin at the hotel. We don't know who the guy reported to, or who knows about Devin. Our whole deal could be blown. One thing's for sure; we've got two major players here.

"Let's knock off; I need some time to think and I want to have Clark's code book copied before I send it back to D.C. If Clark has anything to do with what's going on at Berkeley, we may never know what's in that book."

"I hope you know what you're doin', Barry. If the boss finds out you're copying codebooks, he'll have your ass."

"I'll be careful." Keys cocks his head toward two FBI men at the far end of the room; he does not bother to lower his voice. "If our brother agents would share some information instead of all this secret crap, you know what I mean, 'The need to know'. Aw hell, we've been through all this; how 'bout a beer on the way home?"

Keys stumbles getting up from his desk chair; he sits back down massaging his leg. "Or maybe I'll just go home and get some shuteye."

Chapter 21

Nick feels relieved to be back at Mare Island. Even on a Sunday the tempo of getting the *Bullshark* ready for sea trials is speeding up. Captain Shaver now has all of his officers and most of his sailors back from leave. He holds a meeting of all the available men to talk about the improvements made to the boat.

Shaver lauds the improvements to rally the men's enthusiasm. He tells them that along with the advances in radar and sonar, the new thicker, high-tensile-strength steel hull will allow the *Bullshark* to operate at previously unheard-of depths. Where the sea will permit, the new boat can dive beyond six hundred feet. He reminds the men this feature could put their boat below the explosions of Japanese depth charges by as much as two hundred feet.

Shaver reveals his plan, saying that the new radar will enable the sub's crew to more precisely plot their attack. This will be a huge advantage as it will allow the sub's greater surface speed to find and track the Japanese without them being aware.

Shaver's inspired talk instills a renewed confidence among the men. Most of the men are now anxious to get back in the war. Shaver ends the gathering with a rousing, "I'm making sure that our boat has the best of everything. We've got all the latest gadgets, best radar, best guns, best torpedoes. Our *Bullshark* is the finest submarine in the world, made by the most dedicated men and women in the world.

"Not only that, but, thanks to our cook, Moe, and Chief Devin, we've got the best ice cream too. The job's up to us now. So, together we need to sink ships to starve the enemy, and get this war over with."

Nick, along with the other sixty-plus men, gives an enthusiastic cheer before filing out of the building. Walking back to the boat, Nick jokes with his shipmates; he is feeling refreshed, happy. The smells of water and diesel wash away the intrigues he has no control over. Almost to the boat he feels someone tugging on the back of his shirt.

"Oh, hi, Doris. What are you doing here on a Sunday?"

"I want to talk to you, Nick."

"You got your point across, Doris."

"Look, Nick, I'm sorry. Please just come over to the office with me for a moment, I want you to understand."

"I'm on duty, Doris. I can't just walk off."

Nick sees Captain Shaver walking toward them.

"What's cookin', Chief?" the captain asks.

"I was just telling Doris that I'm on duty, sir."

Doris steps in front of Nick, facing Shaver. "I just need a few minutes of Nick's time, Captain."

"Take a few, Chief; I'll see you on board."

"Um, thank you, sir," Nick says solemnly.

No one is in the office when Nick and Doris arrive.

"Nick, I am so sorry for the things I said. It was just all the stress and the beating from that gorilla,

Dieter. Please forgive me, Nick; I need you to be my friend."

Nick looks at the frail little woman shaking his head. "It's okay, Doris, we're friends, there's nothing to forgive."

Doris puts her arms around Nick, hugging him to her tightly.

A vicious blow to the side of his head sends Nick crashing to the floor. Nick gets to his hands and knees, hearing a scream that seems distant. Taking a moment to clear his head he realizes that the scream was from Doris. Dieter is slapping her face repeatedly.

"I told you to stay away from the sailor boy. I oughta kill you," Dieter yells in Doris' face.

Doris' eyes go wide and Dieter turns to see Nick getting to his feet. Dieter grabs Doris' hair in his left hand. "Stay right where you are, Devin. You shoulda minded your own business. This is between the woman and me."

Nick steps forward testing his balance. Dieter balls his fist to hold it in front of Doris. "You want to watch me learn this bitch a lesson? Stay back!"

Nick's face turns to a deadly grimace. Dieter takes a step back, pulling Doris with him. Nick does not advance. Dieter smirks, then punches Doris hard in her stomach. Doris falls to her knees, pulling free from Dieter's grip. Nick leaps forward in a blind rage swinging a roundhouse right at Dieter's head.

Dieter staggers back trying to dodge the fist, struggling to get a gun from his pocket. Nick's blow clips Dieter's jaw without much power. Before Dieter can get the gun from his pocket Nick has his hands around Dieter's throat. They both crash back to the floor, Nick staying on top.

He straddles Dieter's chest with his knees, pinning Dieter's arms. Nick rears back, and begins to pummel the man's head and face with heavy blows from both fists. Blood flies from Dieter's nose and split lips. Nick continues to punch.

Nick feels something thumping on his back. He hears Doris screaming for him to stop. He can't stop. Doris falls to his side grabbing at his arms.

"Stop it, stop it. You're going to kill him. Nick stop!"

Doris struggles to wedge herself between the two men.

Nick has to stop to keep from hitting Doris. He looks at the man on the floor as if seeing him for the first time. Dieter's eye lids are lumps of angry purple flesh already swelling up. Splattered blood covers the rest of his face. Nick looks from Dieter's broken face to his own fists as if they belong to someone else.

"Jesus Christ, this has gotta end. I can't do this anymore."

Doris' face comes into focus. "We can't stop now, Nick. We've got to get Benny back first. Please don't quit on me now, we're so close. Please Nick, please."

Nick gets to his feet. "I'll go find a guard."

"No!" Doris shouts. "You go get cleaned up and go back to your ship. I'll take care of this."

"How the hell are you gonna take care of Dieter? If he's not dead, he sure ain't gonna walk outta here. You can't get him off the island by yourself."

Doris stands in front of Nick, her dress spotted with blood. "He's not dead, Nick. I can get Dieter's car;

he parks off Third Street. I'll go get it and back it up to the door if you'll help me get him in the back. We can't let the guards find him. Smith's monsters will kill Benny if we let Dieter get caught. I'll get the car, okay, Nick?"

"Okay, go get the car."

Pulling a coat on over her bloodstained dress, Doris rushes out.

Nick goes back to look at Dieter. He is relived to see the man's chest move. He bends down to get the gun out of Dieter's pocket and notices the Mare Island worker's badge on his shirt. Nick tugs on the badge but the badge has a clasp on the back of it.

"You're not ever gettin' back on this yard if I can help it," Nick mutters. He rips the badge off the man's shirt, pulls the clasp apart and tucks the bloody strip of shirt back in Dieter's pocket.

A few minutes later Doris comes in. Together she and Nick get Dieter to the office door. Doris makes sure the coast is clear and they put Dieter on the floor in the back of the car. She covers the bloody body with a dark, thick wool blanket.

Doris turns to Nick, "I'll go back in and clean up the office now. I'll get Dieter back to the house in Crockett; the other man was there when I left. He should know what to do. Go get cleaned up, Nick. Don't tell anyone about this.

"Please, Nick. Just get Smith what he wants and we'll be done. I'll get Benny back and I'll never trouble you again. I promise, Nick, I promise."

Nick walks back to his barracks to wash off Dieter's blood. Avoiding his own image in the mirror at the wash basin he stares at his hands. The water stings his swollen red knuckles. Changing his shirt and pants he heads back to the *Bullshark*. Dark thoughts keep running through his mind.

Nick grips Dieter's metal badge in his hand, the hard edges biting into his palm. He detours to the north end to find a clearing between ships on the water. Activity is slower here; no one takes any notice of him. Nick takes the pistol from his pants pocket and drops it off the dock making a small splash. Throwing sidearm, Dieter's badge sails out: he throws it as far out into the Mare Island Strait as he can.

Chapter 22

Monday morning when Walsh enters the FBI office he can tell by the look on Keys' face that all is not well. He stops in front of Keys' desk.

"So, what's the story?"

Keys looks up from his desk rubbing his chin.

"I've gotta go out to Mare and hold the kid's hand."

Walsh leans on the desk. "I thought we weren't callin' him the kid."

"Yeah, well, I'm pissed," Keys replies. "Dammit, he lost his head and maybe killed Smith's boy, Dieter."

Walsh's eyes go big. "What! How the hell did that happen?"

"Devin called me last night to tell me he was attacked by the Dieter guy at an office on Mare. He said he was talking to Doris when Dieter hit him from behind and when he got off the floor Dieter was beating on Doris. So Devin jumps on Dieter and beats his face in until Doris stops him."

"Why does he think Dieter's dead?" Walsh asks.

"I asked him the same question. He said when he got to Dieter he was thinking of killing him. He doesn't remember how many times he hit the guy, only that when Doris tried to stop him he couldn't stop.

Apparently she wedged herself between them enough that he had to stop.

"Doris got Dieter's car and she and Devin put him in the back, covered him with a blanket and she drove off to Crockett. Devin says Dieter was barely breathing when they put him in the car. I doubt Smith will take any chances on getting Dieter to a hospital. If the guy's too bad to heal himself, my bet is he'll be sleeping in the ocean with an anchor around his neck."

Walsh slaps the desk. "So what's this gonna do to us? That damned kid! He just doesn't get it, or doesn't care."

Keys is looking off into space in thought. He refocuses on Walsh. "I get that Nick's frustrated. He sees his sub's getting close to trials and he's tired of all the intrigue. Maybe he's scared of missing out of the first patrol. Dieter rode him hard and I think Nick seeing Doris take a beating was enough to set him off."

Keys' face brightens. "But you know, now that I think about it, we can use this. Smith's down a man; let's put some more pressure on him. Nick can tell Smith he was approached by another man for radar information. Smith may know he's got competition with the Reds. If we can force him to rush his game maybe we can find where the dope goes. We'll arrest Smith and squeeze him 'til he gives up everyone involved.

"I was just daydreamin' about arrestin' the guy. He'll know he's up for the electric chair and may think he's got nothin' to lose. But you know there are worse things than gettin' fried."

Walsh looks at Keys with a puzzled frown. "Worse things like what?"

"Take a man like Smith who uses women to get what he wants, a real lady killer. He's got no real loyalties but to himself. How 'bout we put him in a nice private cell with a slob that likes men for a couple a days. Now he can play the feminine part. How long you think he'll hold out on us?"

"As far as your grand plan, I'll tell you, Keys, you have a very devious mind; but I like it, man. A guy like Smith would sell his mother for the rich life. I'll be there to watch him fry if I have anything to say about it. I see you're off the hard feelings about the kid, softy. I mean you're back to callin' him Nick."

"Yeah, yeah, softy, that's me alright. Yeah, you know me, Jer. Ah well, hell, I kinda admire him, the guy's smart and he's tough. He puts his life on the line in a glorified sewer pipe for God and country. He had a way out but he volunteered. I know we get jazzed chasin' the bad guys; this is our war right here. His war is out in the Pacific fightin' Japs and we're keepin' him from it.

"I'm gonna head out to Mare. Actually I'm gonna meet Nick at a bar in Vallejo. He doesn't want his captain to find out about his fight with Dieter. See what you can find on that bread van. I'd like to know why Smith uses that instead of a local car. If you need more dope on it, talk to the boss and have him get one of the L.A. guys to go to El Centro. I need you here, Jerry. I have a feeling that when things pop here it's gonna be big."

Walsh swings his forefinger above his head. "I've got the beat daddy, eight to the bar."

"Righto zoot, you're cookin' with gas." Keys heads for the office door, giving Walsh a backhanded wave. "See you later, Jer."

Keys arrives in the afternoon and finds a parking space by one of the many saloons that line both sides of Georgia Street in the old section of Vallejo. Every bar on the street is doing a brisk business. Various examples of Navy and Marine hats flood the street. Keys orders a beer at the bar, looking over the place for Nick. He hustles to a table in a small booth when three sailors shove off to find some new adventures at the next bar.

Keys, on his second beer, drums his fingers on the table. Nick enters the bar, waves at Keys and orders a beer. Nick points at his beer glass using sign language to overcome the din to see if Keys wants one. The agent shakes his head no. Taking a seat across the table from Keys, Nick apologizes for being late.

"Thanks for meeting me here, Barry. I had to finish some work on the boat before I could go."

"It's okay, Nick. I didn't have to wait long. I needed to talk to you anyway."

Nick takes a long drink of his beer. He puts the mug down, watching the foam slide back down the inside of the glass. He addresses Keys without raising his head.

"Barry, I just can't do anymore. I almost killed that guy and if Doris hadn't stopped me I would have. My boat is almost ready for sea trials."

Nick raises his head to look Keys in the eyes.

"I will not miss her first patrol. My captain and my shipmates are depending on me. I won't let them down.

The only way you can stop me is to throw me in jail or kill me."

"Hold on, Nick! No one's gonna kill you, or put you in jail. This job you're doin' for us is for your shipmates. It is for your boat. If we let these guys get away, they'll continue to mine our secrets and that will lead directly to killin' men and sinkin' boats. That's why the spies are tryin' to get our dope, so they can win the war. I've talked to Captain Shaver. He's okay with one more bite at Smith."

"Ah Jesus, Barry, he hasn't said anything to me. You didn't tell him about Dieter, did you? If that gets out I'm done."

"I didn't tell Shaver anything. I just asked that you be allowed to do one more drawing session with Smith. I told him it would be over with after you do this for me. He wasn't happy but you can draw out the whole schematic for Smith and call it done.

"It will be dangerous. I don't think Smith is gonna want you alive after he gets what he wants. With that in mind I brought some protection for you: I've got an ankle gun for you. It's a small automatic with a holster that you strap around your ankle. I'm gonna have my best men follow you to where Smith is holed up. We'll be in place when you need us.

"I want you to tell Smith about communist spies trying to buy the radar information from you. I want to rattle him. If we can make him rush his contacts, we'll be able to find how he gets the dope out. We'll let the contacts get the dope back to Germany, then bust all of them. You do this last bit and you can be on your boat and off to sink Japs. Sound good?"

"The part about being on my boat sounds good. I really don't want to do anymore of your spy-work at all. You tellin' me I'm probably gonna have to shoot my way outta Smith's could be better."

"That's the stuff, kid. I knew I could count on you. So how do you want to contact Smith?"

"Who the hell you callin' kid? I'm a chief petty officer in the United States Navy, and doin' your dirty work."

"Okay, okay, I'm sorry Nick. It's more a term of ah… friendship. I'm just glad you're on the team. I…"

Nick waves both hands signaling Keys to stop talking. "Now don't get maudlin on me, old man."

Keys' fist tightens on the handle of his beer mug. "Are you tryin' to piss me off?"

Nick smiles back at Keys. "Exactly… my friend. Tell me, Barry, if I'm so important to you, why aren't you the one following the car that takes me to Smith?"

"It's just like your Admirals, Nick, someone has to stand back and coordinate the effort. In this case that's my job. I will be there when you need me. I promise you'll get on your boat in time to get back to your war."

"You mean if I don't get filled fulla lead by Smith and his boys."

Keys shakes his head. "I wouldn't be surprised to see bullets bounce off you like Superman. You've heard the saying only the good die young. I've always heard sailors are the worst rabble rousers in the military and submariners are the worst of the lot."

Nick laughs. "It is a well-deserved distinction. We do work hard to maintain our reputation. I gotta hit the head, I'll be right back."

Nick is washing his hands at the sink when something prods his back. He shakes the water from his hands and starts to turn to his right.

From behind Nick comes a heavily-accented voice. "Do not turn around."

Nick looks up into the mirror. At first he does not see anyone. Then a movement in the reflection shows a small bald man peering around Nick's shoulder.

"Is this a joke? Who put you up to this, Keys?" Nick says into the mirror. "You're a little short for heavy work aren't you?"

Nick feels the pistol barrel jabbed into his back. The foreign voice speaks. "This pistol is to make me the bigger man here."

"Look, Mac, I don't carry much cash..."

"I do not want this cash. I am wanting to find comrade Clark. I wait for you many days here where drinks are. I can not get on ship work yard. You will tell me where comrade Clark is. I have car to take you where I find what you know."

Nick looks in the mirror at the little man, noting the man's nervousness. "Buddy, do you think you're gonna walk me outta this place? There's fifty sailors out there, all I have to do is yell."

"You will not yell; I will shoot."

"You shoot me out there and those sailors will tear you apart. You better give me that gun before one of us gets hurt."

Nick can see indecision clouding the little man's eyes. Two sailors bang the bathrooms door open to stagger in. The little man's eyes go big; he turns his pistol toward the intruders. Nick turns, grabs the man's wrist, then wrenches the gun out of his hand. Holding the man by his shirt Nick stuffs the gun in his pocket, balls his right fist and cocks his arm. The little man shrinks back. Nick hesitates, Dieter's bloody face looming before him. The little man sees the look in Nick's face and straightens.

"Hey buddy," exclaims one of the sailors. "What's goin' on?"

Nick goes behind the little man and hooks his arm around the man's neck. "The little guy tried to roll me. Can you believe the nerve of this guy? He musta thought I was too drunk to put up a fight."

The two sailors advance. "Lets show him how we treat thievin' little jerks."

"Stand down, boys," Nick says. "I'm gonna take real good care a this guy myself."

Nick hustles the man past the sailors. He goes to the booth where Keys sits and shoves the little man down in the seat, then slides in beside him, locking the man in.

Keys looks at the two men in some confusion.

Covering the pistol with his hand Nick pushes it across the table to Keys. "This man wants to know where his comrade Clark is. I thought maybe you could help him out."

Chapter 23

Keys takes the revolver to his lap where it is hidden from view by the table. He swings the cylinder out, removing the bullets, puts the rounds in his coat pocket and sets the gun down on the seat by his hip.

Looking up, Keys asks Nick, "Who the hell is this guy?"

"He's the man that just tried to kidnap me in the bathroom. He says he wants to find his comrade pal Clark. Is Clark the guy from the hotel?"

Key ignores Nick's question, focusing his attention on the little man instead. In a low voice he says, "I am an FBI agent and you are under arrest. What is your name and who are you working for?"

The little man looks at Keys without meeting the agent's eyes, the Adams apple bobbing in his throat. "I am Mikhail. I come from Canada and must now be prisoner of war. I can say no more. Please to tell me of comrade Clark."

Keys leans forward, getting his face closer to the little spy. "Oh, brother, you're gonna tell me a lot more or you're gonna fry in the electric chair. Spying in war time is signing your own death warrant. If you tell me who you report to I may be able to help you."

"I can say nothing. You must take me to be shooted. No frying for prisoner of war."

"Mikhail, if you don't talk to me, you'll be strapped down in a wooden chair and thousands of volts of electricity will jolt through your body. Your hair will catch on fire; you'll smell the smoke from your brain frying while you pull and twist at the straps that tie your arms and legs down. Believe me, it's a horrible death; I've been to San Quentin's death chamber. The only chance you've got is to tell me every thing you know."

Nick and Keys both look at the little spy who sits quietly, head bowed, tears running down his cheeks. He straightens in the chair, knuckling away his tears. "I can tell you nothing because that is all I know. My—you call job I think—to make reports Clark says. I make reports put them in package to leave where instructions say leave. I see nobody, just leave reports."

"A dead drop," Keys says. "Okay, Mikhail, that's a start. Where did you receive your training?"

Mikhail speaks in a low voice. Keys strains to hear. "I not train for this. I work in office making words on machine." He holds his hands out fingers splayed and moving as if typing. "Bosses send me here. They take wife and son, tell me go, do what they say or never see wife and son ever. Now I caughted, I not care; life no more for me, wife and boy son."

Keys puts Mikhail's gun in his pocket. "Nick, I've got to get this man back to headquarters. Call me tomorrow so I can fill you in on the next step. Can you make the Smith contact?"

Nick looks at the little man, then answers Keys, "Five by five, Barry."

Nick calls Keys the next evening to confirm his instructions for his final meeting with Smith. "I set it up with Doris when I got back to Mare yesterday. I passed by her office after I finished work; she says I'll be picked up at the same place this Saturday morning."

"Good work, Nick. We'll be done soon. Do me a favor and walk around a little with that ankle gun I gave you. If you favor that leg it's a dead giveaway. You need to get used to it, okay?

"You want me to practice my quick draw too? I'm glad I don't have a lotta time to worry about this. Just make sure this is the last time, Barry. Next week we begin the first sea trials. That's all I want to think about. If I make one stupid mistake, the whole boat suffers.

"I know it's important to you, Barry; I'll do my part. The best thing is that it'll be over with soon, no more secret agent crap. I'll be able to have a beer in a bar without some nitwit pokin' a gun in my back. I do kinda feel sorry for that little Mikhail guy. Sounds like he was forced into the job. God knows he sure wasn't a tough guy. Did you get anymore out of him?"

Keys hesitates on his end of the phone line. "We'll never know much about what he did or how he got into it, Nick. He found you from what our roof-flying friend Clark had doped out. He typed that up in a report he dropped. But he was depressed enough, and tough enough, to hang himself in his cell last night."

"You're in a lousy line of business, Barry."

"Same could be said of your job, Nick. War is the worst of humanity. We never learn. Listen up. I want you to be careful at Smith's. Anytime you feel threatened get to a window and light a cigarette. That will be the signal you want to get out of there. I'll have my guys surrounding the house on the lookout for the flare of your cigarette."

Keys pauses a moment searching for some better assurance to give to Nick.

"If you have to, break a window, or just pull the curtains open and shut; do anything to make a signal. Hell, I don't care, you can set the damned place on fire. In any case I'll be there; you can bank on it."

Chapter 24

Nick steps across the ferry landing to cross The Embarcadero and on to the rail yard. On the far side of the rail yard he sees the black bread van with Willi leaning on the front fender smoking a cigarette. On the other side of the car is a man Nick doesn't recognize. Willi says something to the man Nick can't hear; the man gets in the passenger seat of the van.

Willi flips his cigarette to the street and opening the van doors motions Nick to the rear. The interior of the van is as dark and smelly as Nick remembers. The doors slam shut behind him. He quickly finds a wooden milk crate to sit on in a corner before the van pulls away.

The first team of agents follows the van at a distance down The Embarcadero toward the Bay Bridge. Willi drives, keeping pace with the moderate traffic across the bridge where the second FBI team picks up the tail. The FBI men fall back thinking that Willi will be headed to the same Berkeley address they took Nick to before.

When the van turns off San Pablo Avenue onto Dwight Way the FBI men are alerted that the van is headed to a different location. They close up on the van as they come to a traffic light. The van speeds up to make the light, going through on the yellow. The FBI men have to stop behind the two cars ahead of them.

The van disappears down Dwight Way as the FBI man drums his fingers on the steering wheel. The traffic light seems to take an eternity to change. The driver of the car at the light is not paying attention and doesn't move when the light changes. Frustrated the FBI man pounds the steering wheel, then the horn. "It doesn't get any greener, you idiot!"

The FBI agent in the passenger seat chimes in with his frustration. "What the hell's the matter with these dumb jerks? I don't get it; they must think the car drives itself."

The FBI driver pulls around the car in front of him swearing at the other driver who is fiddling with the car's radio tuner.

"Pay attention to traffic for Christ's sake," he yells. After getting through the light the FBI men scour the road ahead; the bread van is nowhere in sight.

Willi turns down California Street, going for several blocks to turn into a driveway of a weathered two-story house. The old clapboard house is on a large unkempt lot set back from the street. Twin strips of concrete driveway choked with weeds end at the back side of the house. A dirt path winds around in back of the house past a chicken coop to a small barn. Willi parks the van inside a ramshackle barn and shuts off the engine. Nick blinks in the strong sunshine when the van's rear doors open.

"Get out and follow Rodolfo," Willi growls.

Nick looks at the tall Hispanic man. "Who's this? Where's Dieter?"

Willi, gun drawn, pushes Nick forward. "You'll pay for Dieter, sailor boy; get in the house before I kick your ass."

Rodolfo opens the door and stands aside as Nick enters. "Put your arms out to your sides," he orders.

Nick turns toward the voice and is roughly turned back. Rodolfo spreads Nick's arms to expertly pat down his body. He finishes with Nick's upper torso, then goes down each leg from the crotch. Rodolfo finds the gun Keys gave Nick at the right ankle. He triumphantly holds the little automatic up for Willi to see.

Willi grabs the gun from Rodolfo. "You son of a bitch! What'd you think you were gonna do with that pea shooter? You gonna kill all us, finish the job you started with Dieter? You ain't…"

Smith rushes into the room. "What are you yelling about?"

Willi holds up the gun. "Sailor boy here's got a little pistol. Looks like he's got plans to kill us all."

"Where did you get the pistol?" Smith asks.

"I got it from a friend at Mare. I thought I might need it if more of you spies showed up."

"More spies from where? What are you talking about?" Smith queries.

"A guy offered me a ton a money for the same thing you're after, said he knew all about your setup," Nick replies.

Smith steps closer to Nick, looking agitated. "What guy, who was he? I mean, what did he look like? Who does he represent?"

"I don't know who he is. He's a big guy, real short grey hair. He sounds maybe Polish or Russian or something."

Smith's eyes narrow as he turns angrily to Willi. "Wilhelm, did anyone follow you here?"

"I didn't see anyone. How 'bout you, Rudy?"

"I asked you, Wilhelm," Smith growls.

"No sir, I didn't see anyone following us, sir."

Smith takes the gun from Willi. "Rudy, keep a lookout from the front of the house. Wilhelm show Mr. Devin to the blackboard; we must complete this."

"Excuse me, Mr. Smith," Rodolfo interjects. "Willi should be the one to stand watch. As you may remember, I was sent to be your number two and to report to our superiors. The man Devin describes is similar to the man I reported to you. You said no one else had reported anyone suspicious. "

Smith spins around, Nick's pistol in his hand. He gives Rodolfo a long hard look, the muscles in his jaws working. Rodolfo unflinchingly stands his ground. Smith breaks off the staring match. "Yes, of course. Rudy, you are correct. Willi, you will pay if you have failed me! Now go watch the front! Devin, follow me."

Nick follows Smith up a flight of stairs into another room. There are two lights directed to a blackboard on a wall. The one large window in the room has a plywood panel hastily nailed to the wall covering the window. Nick thinks the cigarette signal Keys set up is not going to work.

"Now get to it, Devin," Smith barks. "Do not waste any more of my time. I want it all now."

Nick goes to the board, picks up a stick of chalk and begins to draw.

Chapter 25

A half mile north of Smith's place both of the FBI teams tasked with following Smith's van have called into headquarters to say they have lost contact. Headquarters relays the number Keys gave them to contact him.

"Goddamnit," Keys roars, pounding the shelf of the phone booth. "Go find him! I want both teams to cover every street in a ten block radius from where you lost him. Report back by car radios."

"But sir, you said not to be on the radio; what if they overhear us?"

"That's just what I want; if we can't find him maybe we can buy him some time. Now get to it, check all parking lots and driveways. If you see anything of the van, or something suspicious, radio me immediately."

Keys returns to the car Walsh has idling at the curb.

"They lost him," Keys says getting into the car.

"What do you want to do, Barry?" Walsh asks.

Keys stares out into space for a moment before answering.

"Let's find the local cop shop; radio headquarters and ask where it is, will you?"

With the screech of worn brakes that sends Keys forward in the seat, Walsh brings the car to a halt in front of the police station.

Inside the well-worn station, Keys pulls out his FBI identification to show the cop on the front counter. "I need to talk to your captain."

The precinct captain, a burly hirsute man with black tufts of hair spouting from his collar, comes from his office to see what the FBI man wants.

"What can I do you for, bud?" the captain asks, neglecting a handshake.

Keys puts his I.D. away. "I would be grateful if you would put out a radio call to your cars for this vehicle we're looking for."

"You askin' or tellin'?" the captain barks.

Keys' face goes hard before he takes a breath. "I am politely asking for your assistance in a matter that is of great importance to our war effort... sir."

The captain sees his officers gathering to take notice of the two men. He steps forward hands on hips to face down Keys. "You feds always want something but you never give nothin' back."

"Captain, I don't have time for this; this is an emergency. I'll say please, I'd appreciate your help. If that doesn't do it for you, I'll make a quick call to Washington and bring the federal government down on your head like a ton a bricks."

The captain takes a step back. "All right, because we're all doin' what we can to win this war, and 'cause you said please, tell the radioman what you want." He points to a door behind the counter.

"Thank you." Keys nods, taking out his notepad as he heads toward the door.

Back with Walsh in the car he briefly describes his encounter with the police.

"Anyway, they're radioing now, that's what I wanted. Let's try to make something happen here.

"Damn it." Keys slaps the hard steel dashboard. "I promised Devin he'd sail on his new sub. You know Smith or Seidel, whatever you want to call him, has no plan to let Nick go. If we don't find him, he's a dead man."

Walsh looks over at Keys, his face grim, narrowing his eyes.

Keys shakes his head at Walsh's look. "Okay, okay. So our teams lost him several blocks down Dwight Way. Let's go to the first tall building you see. I'll go to the top of the building and use the binoculars from the trunk to scan the area. We'll take a few square blocks at a time and see if anything pops out."

Getting out of the car, Keys bends down to look back under the roof line at Walsh. "Stay with the radio, Jerry. Come get me if you hear anything from our teams."

The first tall building they come to is only a three-story rooming house. Keys finds there is no elevator in the place and has to walk up the flights of stairs, further punishing his leg. At the top flight he massages his leg, lamenting that he is out of the vet's pain pills.

Chapter 26

Nick works at the blackboard, sometimes erasing a line to add another feature or to correct a symbol, stalling for time. Smith fidgets at his desk growing more and more impatient, drumming his pen while staring at Nick's back.

Willi bursts into the room. "The van's on the police radio! They got the license number an' everything."

Smith jumps up from his desk chair. "Verdammit! What is it, Willi? You are to be watching the front of this place."

"I went to the radio room for my cigarettes, and turned the radio on to listen to the police band. They're lookin' for the van. They've got the license number and the registration."

Smith's face flushes red as an angry vein thumps on his forehead. "I gave you an order, you dummkopf. You and your idiot cousin Dieter have ruined my work. All the meticulous planning I put into this mission only to have you put the enemy onto us!"

"Take it easy, boss," Willi exclaims. "If I hadn't tuned the radio to the police band we wouldn't a known they knew about the van. I done a good thing for us."

Nick watches the exchange between Smith and Willi over his shoulder. It is the first time he has seen Smith rattled. Tension fills the room. To his right he notes that the Hispanic man, Rodolfo, remains calm. He motions to Nick to turn around and continue his work on the blackboard.

Smith snatches Nick's automatic from his desk top, jams it in a pocket, then opens a desk drawer to remove his Luger pistol. With the Luger clutched in his hand he rushes to leave the room.

Nick sneaks a look at Rodolfo; the man has taken in every event with a bemused, almost smiling look on his face. Nick's faint hope of being forgotten in the confusion is dashed when Smith stops at the door with an order for Willi.

"Lock the sailor up downstairs."

Willi, still stinging from Smith's anger, points his thumb at Rodolfo. "What's the Mex gonna do boss?"

Before Smith replies, Rodolfo says, "The Mex is going to remain calm and make sure the barn is secured, dummkopf. Did you think to close the doors? You should concern yourself with the orders your boss gave you."

Willi pulls a pistol from his pocket. "He's your boss too, greaser."

Smith ducks back out of the room on his way to a room at the end of the landing with a window view of the street.

Rodolfo slowly shakes his head. "If you point that pistol at me, arschloch, you're a dead man."

Willi hesitates, then looks away from Rodolfo. He prods Nick with the barrel of his pistol. "Come on, sailor boy."

Nick starts down the landing to the stairs, Willi pushing him along with the barrel of his gun. At the head of the stairs Nick turns his head to mutter over his shoulder, "You yellow, Willi?"

Willi shoves Nick hard, sending the sailor tumbling down the stairs. Nick hits the floor at the foot of the stairs expelling his breath with a loud oof. His arms splayed, he lays motionless face down, his right leg bent at the knee under him.

Rodolfo looks down over the banister to see Nick sprawled on the floor. Willi goes down the stairs toward Nick. "Did you kill him? He didn't finish the radar diagram, you know. The boss won't be happy."

Rodolfo turns back to the blackboard room, taking a notebook from his pocket. Willi cautiously prods Nick with the toe of his shoe, then bends down to feel for a pulse.

Nick springs up on his right leg and smashes down on Willi's head with a vicious blow from his right fist. Willi drops to the floor like a bag of bones. Nick drags him to a closet and opens the door to roughly stuff Willi in. Nick looks around the room to find a chair he can wedge under the closet's doorknob.

The closest chair he finds is a heavy worn-fabric relic. It screeches across the floor as he struggles to pull it over to the closet door. As Nick bends down to retrieve Willi's pistol, Rodolfo's head appears over the banister. "Drop the gun, Devin!"

Nick dives behind the chair as Rodolfo fires; two bullets thud into the heavy upholstery just above his head. Nick snaps off two shots over the chair. Rodolfo screams in agony, his gun flying over the banister then clattering to floor below. Nick peeks up over the chair at Rodolfo. One of Nick's shots gouged splinters of wood from the banister. Rodolfo has both hands covering his face. Nick sees a wood splinter protruding through Rodolfo's bloody fingers.

Rodolfo slumps back against the wall. Nick rushes across the room, picks up Rodolfo's gun and starts to the stairs. Smith cautiously sticks his head out of his doorway. He sees Rodolfo shaking, blood soaking the front of him. "My god, what's happened?" he cries.

Smith looks over the banister to see Nick going toward the stairs. He fires his Luger, the bullet strikes the floor a few inches in front of Nick. The sailor changes course to jump under the cover of the landing above. Smith fires four more rounds blindly over the banister.

Now just a few blocks east of Nick, Keys comes back to the car from the top of the building he was on. He settles into the car's seat. "Not a damned thing that I can see," he says to Walsh. Their radio crackles and Walsh turns up the volume. Walsh has the radio tuned to the local police band frequency. The message is loud and clear. "Shots fired reported at 2521 California Street, cars two and six respond."

Keys spreads a map against the dashboard to jab his finger to the California Street address. "That's gotta be it. Call our two teams; tell 'em to meet us there. Stand on it, Jer. I wanta beat the cops there. I don't want that boy killed."

Walsh revs the car's engine hard, dumps the clutch only to have the car lurch forward, then stall. Walsh grinds the starter. "Damn these pieces of…"

Keys, his shoulders hunched up, staring straight ahead, yells, "Jerry, get this crate goin' now!"

***

Nick searches for a way out from under the landing; the two doors he finds leading to the rear of the house are locked or sealed shut. Smith hears Nick moving beneath the landing. The Nazi spy holds the Luger out, stretching over the banister to get under the landing and fires three more rounds. With his pistol empty, Smith goes back to his desk to reload the Luger.

Rodolfo staggers toward the stairs. He reluctantly takes one blood smeared hand from his face to feel for the banister. Nick hears heavy footfalls on the stairs and looks out to see Rodolfo painfully making his way down the stairs.

Staying under the landing, Nick calls out Rodolfo. "You'd better stay here 'til the FBI shows up."

Rodolfo turns toward Nick's voice. Nick is startled to see a three inch long splinter stuck in Rodolfo's right eye.

"Please get me to a doctor. I can not bear this pain. I can not stand it. Please I will pay you, I have money."

Nick stays under the landing. "You tell me where the boy is and I'll get you to a doctor."

Rodolfo makes it to the bottom of the stairs. "They did not tell me about a boy; I do not know. Please take me to a doctor."

"You'll have to wait for the FBI."

"FBI, are you with the FBI?"

"I'm workin' with 'em," Nick says. "They should be outside now."

"Good, good, I am FBI too. Take me to a doctor now, I order you."

"You're with the FBI?" Nick asks.

"Yes, yes, of course. Please, please take me now."

Smith emerges from the room upstairs. "FBI, who's with the FBI? Rudi, you are FBI?"

"That's what the man said," Nick shouts. "Where's the boy, Smith?"

Smith fires two shots at the sound of Nick's voice. "Rudi, stay where you are," Smith yells.

Rodolfo scrambles toward the front door, crabbing along the wall for support.

"Stop, Rudi, stop!"

Nick fires two bullets overhead through the floor of the landing.

Smith springs backward to fall into a doorway, shocked by the near misses through the floor. Nick hears a thump and thinks he might have hit Smith.

"Bastard, filthy stupid bastard." Badly shaken, Smith gets up from the floor to pound back to the landing in a rage. He fires over the banister and then through the floor. Rodolfo is opening the front door when Smith notices him. Smith fires three rounds and Rodolfo crumples to the ground.

Nick fires two more shots overhead making Smith jump back. "Give it up, Smith, the FBI have the place surrounded."

"I will never give up! You will never take me alive."

"You've been watching too many gangster movies, Smith. Throw your guns down or you will be killed. I don't think you've got the guts to take a bullet."

"You have no FBI. There is only you. Soon my country will wipe your kind from the face of the earth. I will be a hero to my people. If you try anything, I will shoot you like a dog."

"Are you gettin' your nerve back, Smith? How about I burn this place down with you stuck in it?"

Smith fires in the direction of Nick's voice. "If you move I will kill you," Smith roars.

"You must be about outta bullets by now, Smith."

"I have plenty, and your little pistol too, Devin."

"Okay, so you'll burn, Smith. You're gonna fry anyway. You'll die here or you'll die in the electric chair. Either way I'm gonna watch it happen. One last chance, where's the boy? Where is Benny?"

"There is no Benny, you fool," Smith yells, firing more rounds through the floor.

Nick strikes the flint and tosses his cigarette lighter from under the landing to an old overstuffed sofa. The years of wear and solvents used to clean the old piece drink in the lighter's flame. Acrid smoke, then flame, spring from the old fabric. Smith fires repeatedly through the floor. Nick returns the shots with his own from Rodolfo's pistol to keep Smith off balance.

Keys and Walsh both rush from the car as soon as it stops. A small crowd of people are lining the sidewalk outside the Smith house. They hear the shots from within the house and see smoke rising from the open front door. The other two FBI teams screech to a halt in front. The smoke coming from the house spurs Keys to start for the house. Walsh tries to stop him but Keys pulls away.

"Stay put, Jerry; I gotta see if Nick's okay."

Keys makes his way to the front of the house, staying low. Crouching with his knees bent sends a spark of pain from his bad leg. He stays to one side of the open front door, then lies on the porch to look in. He can see Smith on the upper landing and Nick underneath pressed against the wall. Nick moves to one end to fire a shot then scrambles away. Smith returns fire toward the place Nick's shots came from. Keys waves his arm trying to get Nick's attention.

Smith sees Keys first and directs his shots to the front door. Nick, at first confused, turns to see what Smith is shooting at. Keys ducks the shots, then motions Nick to go to the far side of the wall. Nick first thinks Keys is waving at him. Nick gives a jaunty wave back. Nick can almost see the color of Keys' face change. Keys shakes his fist, then motions Nick to move. Devin forms an "O" with his thumb and forefinger to signal Keys the okay sign.

Keys squirms backward out of the front door opening. He stands out of the line of fire and yells into the house. "You're surrounded, Smith. Give up now and you won't be hurt."

"You do not know who you are dealing with," Smith yells back. "The Reich will never allow you to prosecute me. I will never surrender."

"He thinks he's Eddie Robinson in Little Caesar," Nick shouts to Keys.

Smith slams a freshly loaded clip into the butt of his Luger, fires down at Nick, then out the front door. Dirt and wood splinters fly as the bullets hit the front porch.

Keys ducks back, then shouts, "That's the only warning you're gonna get, Smith. We know all about you, Amil Seidel. You've failed at everything you've ever tried and now you're gonna pay."

More shots strike the porch. Keys stays low and makes his way to the cars in front.

Huddled behind the cars, Keys instructs his men. "You two guys go around back and make sure no one gets away. I want two men on the sides of the house and Jerry, make sure no one gets out of the front."

"What are you gonna do?" Walsh asks Keys.

"Clear these people outta the way."

Keys gets into their old Dodge and starts the engine. Grinning at Walsh, Keys shouts, "I'm gonna make a house call."

Keys revs the engine, then slipping the clutch unmercifully to get the reluctant old car going, he drives twenty yards down California Street. Turning around and shifting up through the gears to gain momentum, he makes a wide turn to keep the energy going. The car bounds over the sidewalk and through the rickety old fence sending splintered wood flying. The old Dodge is still gaining speed when Keys hits the shallow porch steps launching a ton and a half of Detroit steel smashing through the front of the clapboard house.

The battered car explodes through woodwork, glass, and furnishings, crashing hard into the rear wall. The upper landing where an astonished Smith stands, collapses on top of the Dodge bringing the Nazi spy down with it.

Chapter 27

Nick ducks back and forth under the landing above him to dodge Smith's frantic gunfire. Bits of plaster and wood fly through the air. The plaster dust falls like snow, reminding Nick of the cork dust in his submarine after a close depth charge attack.

Nick's hearing is dulled by loud cracks of gunfire; he thinks he can hear an engine screaming. Suddenly from outside the front of the house comes a crash. He turns to see, through the open front door, a car flying at the house like a runaway freight train. Wide-eyed, Nick squeezes into a corner staying out of Smith's field of fire and away from the steel monster that smashes through the front of the house.

The car, barely slowed by wood and furniture, thunders into the rear wall a few scant feet from where Nick stands. The wall shatters, plaster and wood flying in all directions. The landing above it, now unsupported, collapses with a loud crack.

Nick jumps past the car as the ledge of the landing crashes to the ground. Smith screams, falling on the back of the car, sliding down the trunk to land face down on the floor in a shower of debris. Nick rushes to get on top of him before he gets up, pulling Smith's arms behind the spymaster's back.

Keys kicks at the car door with his good leg, trying to get out. The Dodge's broken radiator hisses loudly, spewing clouds of steam into the mayhem of billowing dust and debris. Walsh, gun drawn, runs into the house. "Barry, you alright, man?" He waves his hand in front of him trying to see through the clouds of dust.

Nick sees Walsh and yells out to him, "Take care of Smith. I'll help Keys outta the car. I can hear him cursing up a storm tryin' to kick the door open."

Nick clears wood and plaster from the car, then pulls on the driver-side door while Keys pushes with his foot.

"No good, Barry, it's fubar. I'll try the other side." Nick goes to the passenger side. The car is buried on that side deep into rear wall. Nick goes back to the driver's side and yanks on the rear door. Putting his right foot up on the rear fender he pulls hard on the door handle. With screech of tortured metal, the door opens a few inches. Nick gets his hands inside the door frame to pull on the door until he wrenches it open.

Nick expels a breath. "You'll have to climb over the seat and get out the back door."

Keys pulls himself up on the front seat. "Can't you get this damned door open? I ain't exactly a monkey you know."

Nick laughs. "You maybe ain't a monkey but you're crazy as one. If I hadn't seen you comin' you'd a run me over with that tank."

"You're just pissed I had to pull your fat outta the fire again, sailor. Come on, help me outta this crate."

"You got some nerve, Keys, I'll give you that. Where the hell have you guys been? That idiot Smith made swiss cheese outta the floor of the landin' tryin' to kill me. You said you'd be right outside."

Nick gets in the back of the car to help haul Keys over the front seat back.

"Easy man," Keys bellows. "Remember my leg. You know, the one that got a bullet in it savin' your hide."

"Jesus, Keys, did that crash rattle your brain or what? If it wasn't for me you'd be sleepin' in the dirt, man."

"Yeah, well, I damned near killed myself gettin' you outta this mess, my friend." Keys leans on the car's fender to catch his breath after struggling over the seat back and out of the rear door. "Look, Nick, right now we need to get Smith outta here before the locals show up. I don't want them thinkin' he's gonna answer to them. Where's the rest of his gang?"

Nick points to the other side of the room. "Willi's in the closet over there. I don't know where Rodolfo got off to."

Keys, brushing himself off, asks, "Who's Rodolfo? Where's Dieter?"

"Dieter's dead," Nick answers. "Rodolfo's the man that replaced him. I thought Smith killed him. He was lying by the front door a while ago."

"Give Walsh a description of the guy. I'm takin' Smith back to the Bureau with me, Nick. You go on back to Mare with Walsh; I'll talk to you later. You're a pain in the ass, sailor, a good man, but still a pain. I owe you; hell we all owe you. Don't get a big head. Get back to Mare safe, will you?"

Keys helps Walsh get the now-handcuffed Smith to his feet.

"Jerry, get Willi outta the closet and make sure there's no one else on the grounds. Leave a man to take statements from the neighbors and help the local cops look for Rodolfo. See that Nick catches a ferry to Mare and get back to the Bureau as soon as you can. I'll take a car; you can bring Willi and our guys back with you. With any luck the bean counters will send the Dodge to the scrap yard."

By the time Walsh gets back to the San Francisco bureau's headquarters, Keys has been grilling Smith, who they are now officially calling Amil Seidel, for hours.

"Where the hell have you been?" asks Keys.

"Keep your shirt on, Barry. We got caught by the cops before we could leave. I had to do some fancy talking to get us away. Every time they pressed I said national security to the point the police chief told us to clear out before he shot us."

Keys angrily rubs his face. "What about Devin? Did they get on to him?"

"No. When the cops showed I sent him out to the sidewalk to blend in with the rubberneckers. I picked him up down the block when they cut us loose and took him to the ferry so he could get back to the shipyard. Me and the other guys came straight back here. I stuck Willi in a cell with the local P.D. Did you get anything out of Smith?"

"Nah, I beginning to think the guy's nuts. He thinks the Reich is gonna send somebody to spring him. I told him we're at war with Germany, so he says the Mexican authorities will get him out. I tell him Mexico's got no jurisdiction. I don't know if it's an act or what."

Walsh puts his coat on the back of a chair and sits down. "So are you gonna lock him up with some gorilla like you planned?"

"I don't think that's gonna work on this guy, Jerry. He's nuts enough to get himself killed. We need information from this guy. I can't take a chance on him killin' himself, or havin' a con do it. The cons aren't liable to take kindly to a spy, and Seidel would want to tell everyone how brilliant he thinks he is."

"That's too bad; I'd like to see the guy in some hell hole."

Keys snaps his fingers. "Jerry, you've got it. A hell hole. I just read a newspaper article about the dungeons on Alcatraz. I met Jimmy Johnston, the warden, a coupla years ago. The guy's first class. Get us some coffee will ya? I'm gonna make a phone call."

When Walsh comes back with paper cups of coffee, Keys has his feet up on his desk looking pleased with himself.

"You look like a man with a plan," Walsh says.

"Yeah, I gotta plan. See the deal is, I read the inmates think the dungeon's haunted. The warden just told me they don't use 'em anymore; it's too cruel he says. But when I told him about our friend Seidel, he says we can try it for a day or two.

"Get one of our guys Seidel hasn't seen and put him in a holding cell next to our great Nazi spy master. I'll go down and tell Seidel we're takin' him to Alcatraz, where he can rot. You tell our man to play up the haunted deal. The warden says the dungeon cells were built in the 1860's underground. The cells down there drip with moisture and are cold, dark, and lousy with rats.

"He says since they quit using the place the stories about ghosts get more exaggerated. When they used the dungeon they took the prisoner down there, stripped him naked, then threw him in the cell. There's no bed just a wet cold brick floor, ceiling, and walls. There's almost no light when they close the cell's door, and, as it's below ground, there's all kinds a weird noises from the cells upstairs at night.

"After a day or two I'm betting Seidel's gonna open up like a ripe melon. I just wish I could watch him squirm in that dungeon cell. Johnston said men were rumored to go insane down there. Tell our guy to fill Seidel's head with that stuff too."

"I hope that's the case," Walsh says. "How about I get a coupla our guys back to Berkeley after Rodolfo? Nick said the guy's got a wood splinter stickin' out of his right eye and probable gunshot wounds. I don't think he went too far."

"Yeah, sounds good, Jerry. You take care of that and I'll find a man to put in the holding cell next to Seidel."

Keys walks into the holding cell, pushing a man along in front of him. They stop at the cell next to Seidel's; Keys roughly shoves the man into the cell. The sound of the steel door slamming shut rings in the room.

Keys stands in front of Seidel's cell door. "Okay, Seidel, since you've got nothing to say, I've found the perfect place for you to rot. You and me are gonna take a boat ride out to Alcatraz. My friend the warden has agreed to let you feed the rats in one of the dungeon cells. You'll be all alone; they aren't allowed to keep men down there anymore.

165

"I made a special deal for you. The warden hates spies so you can spend the rest of your miserable life in a place worse then hell. If you decide you've got something to tell me after the rats chew on you a while, you better yell real loud. The guards don't pay much attention to anyone yellin' down there."

After Keys leaves, the man in the adjacent cell glances over to Seidel every few minutes until Seidel stares back at him, then snarls, "What are you looking at?"

"Ah, sorry I just was tryin' to figure out who you are. You must be some big trouble for the feds to lock you in an Alcatraz dungeon."

Seidel breathes in, puffing himself up. "I'm bigger than these idiots have ever seen."

Keys' man steps closer to Seidel's cell. "I'll say you must be if they're gonna put you in the dungeon on the Rock. I hear that's the scariest place on earth. Men either die down there or go insane. Friend of mine got sent down there and he ain't been right since."

Seidel gets up from his bunk to get closer to the other man. "What do you mean, he's not right?"

"Ben Carver's the guy. He just stares out at nothin' and mumbles about ghosts and huge rats. Says some dead men tried to steal his soul. The man gives me the willies just lookin' at him."

"Your friend was visited by spirits?" Seidel asks.

"Visited? Hell, man, he was haunted by 'em. He said they'd come right through the walls and when they'd come the rats would run all over the place tryin' to get away from 'em. He showed me the scars on his legs from where the rats tried to eat him, too."

Seidel, looking somewhat deflated, says, "They can not do such things in this country. There must be a due process of law."

"Mister, when the feds want to do something, they throw the law books away. I heard that if the dungeon guards are feelin' mean they won't even feed you. If you die on 'em, when the smell gets too bad they haul your carcass out an' throw it to the sharks. They ain't interested in no due process. No, sir."

Keys enters the holding cell. "Hey, didn't I tell you no talkin' in here?" He shoves a key into the lock of Seidel's door. "Come on, Seidel, we're goin' for a boat ride. Hope you don't get too sea sick; the bay's mighty choppy today. By this time tomorrow you're gonna wish all you had to worry about was bein' seasick."

The bay is cold and overcast. Alcatraz looms out of the fog as the boat reaches the dock. Seidel, who has maintained a silent attitude of defiance throughout the trip, now has trouble finding his feet. Keys helps the handcuffed Seidel up onto the dock, showing the guards his identification. One of the guards looks Seidel over, then grunts, takes him by the arm and says, "Come with me."

Keys says, "Hey, hold up, he's my prisoner."

The second guard says to Keys, "He'll be okay; the warden wants to have a word with you."

The guard escorts Keys to the warden who waits just up the hill from the dock. He comes forward to shake Keys' hand as the first guard and Seidel pass. "Welcome to Alcatraz, Agent Keys. I'll have the guard take you down to your man in just a moment." He turns away and, taking Keys by the arm, walks a few paces away from the second guard.

"I know you're anxious to get your man to talk," the warden says. "And that it is important to our war effort. However, I will not condone undo cruelty. By that I mean beatings, or any form of physical damage. You know that is why we no longer use the dungeon."

Keys nods his understanding. "Yes, sir. I'm hoping that just the threat of his spending the rest of his life in the dungeon will be enough to make him talk."

"You can have two days, maybe three at the outside, to keep him down there. I have directed that his cell have a cot and that he be dressed in a prison uniform. Good luck, agent; if you can let me know how it turns out I would appreciate it."

The warden shakes Keys' hand again and with a wink says, "The guards may have some useful tips for you." Warden Johnston nods to the waiting guard. "Dick will take you to the dungeon entry."

"Thank you, sir, I will let you know how it goes and, on behalf of the FBI, we do appreciate your cooperation."

The guard steps over to Keys. "This way, sir. We have the prisoner waiting."

In cell block A, on the cheerfully named Sunrise Alley, is a three-sided, shoulder-high concrete barrier in the center of the walkway. The concrete walls stand ominously as if guarding a descent into hell. On the open side of the barrier is the mouth of the stairway leading down to the dungeon. Seidel stands beside the guard staring down into the darkness of the stairs. The Nazi agent's stature is much deflated.

Keys arrives with the other guard to escort Seidel down the stairs to the dungeon cells. On the cold floor of the cells Keys gives one of the guards the key to

Seidel's handcuffs. The guard removes the handcuffs and tells Seidel to strip.

Seidel's hard look at the three men fades. "I demand my rights as a prisoner of war."

A bemused Keys watches as one of the guards steps up nose to nose in Seidel's face to address him. "You have no rights here! You were not registered when you were bought in. The FBI has requested that you be kept here anonymously until, I believe the term was... you rot. You have no name or number here. We'll just refer to you as zero. If you resist any orders your privileges of food and water will be revoked. Now strip!"

Chapter 28

The chill from the cold dank concrete is not all that makes Seidel shiver. The humiliation of standing naked, hands covering his shriveled manhood, is draining the last vestige of courage from him. The guards and the smirking FBI man enjoying his degradation make the shame he feels almost unbearable. He can not keep his body from betraying him; the trembling is uncontrollable.

"Turn around and bend over," the guard barks.

Seidel stands shaking as if he can not comprehend. The guard grabs his arm, spins him around, then pushes down on the back of Seidel's neck.

"No contraband, he's clean," the second guard says.

"Turn around and put these on." The guard shoves prison clothes at Seidel's chest. Seidel pulls on long underwear, a blue shirt, and grey pants. The welcomed warmth from the clothes dampens the shivers; however his hands still shake uncontrollably.

The guards lead Seidel down the dim hallway. "Hey, Chuck," one guard says to the other. "Let's call this guy shaky. He's liable to piss himself before we get 'em into the cell."

Seidel is shoved roughly into a cell; the cell door clangs shut leaving him in darkness. Feeling his way to the cot, he sits on the edge putting his head in his hands. "Mein Gott," he moans.

Keys asks the guards if there is anyway Seidel could injure himself in his cell.

"Let's move to the stairway," one of the guards suggests. "Low tones carry down here; the effect in a cell is spooky."

At the stairway the guards confer with Keys. "The warden ordered us to keep a 24-hour watch on your man. We won't feed him today but we will keep a good watch on him. If he doesn't break by morning we'll do our best to spook the guy.

"Sounds from above at night, when it's still down here, are scary enough. If that doesn't do it, cigarette and cigar smoke hangs in the air. A little fanning with a clipboard makes it look like ghosts moving."

"Can he see that from his cell?" Keys asks.

"He can if we use our flashlights right, and that's part of the spook show. I've heard tell some of the real hard cases came outta these cells blubbering like a baby. Your man doesn't look in real good shape now. The warden says we can only hold him for two or three days max. So we'll step up the act if he doesn't break soon enough."

Keys shakes hands with the guards. "Thanks, men. I'll check in regularly. This is important, I appreciate your help."

Agent Keys has a message waiting at headquarters the next morning. He picks it up at his desk to read his man on Alcatraz is ready to talk. Keys calls Warden Johnston's office. "Good morning, Warden. Yes, thank you, I just got your message. Could you have a man tell Seidel I will only arrange a leave from your prison if he is prepared to answer all of my questions? He will have to answer all my questions there on Alcatraz."

Less than ten minutes after the first call Keys receives a second phone call from Alcatraz. The message from the warden's assistant is that Seidel refuses to talk until he is taken off the island. "He's afraid you'll leave him in the dungeon after he talks," the assistant says. In a lower voice the man says, "The guards asked me to tell you to leave it to them."

"I'll do just that," Keys replies. "Thank you."

Walsh calls in. "We found Rodolfo. He's in a bad way, I've got him at Highland Hospital. I don't think he's gonna make it. He was lying in some brush two doors down from Seidel's place. When I got him in the car to take him to the hospital all he wanted was to get Seidel. He said he was sent from Mexico to find out how much money Seidel was stealing from German intelligence.

"I can't believe the guy's still breathing. He says the radar dope was the best thing Seidel ever came up with."

Keys sits up in his chair. "Jerry, see if you can find the conduit Seidel was using to get his dope out. I'd like to get Nick's last drawing sent."

"I'll try, Barry. Rodolfo won't last long."

Keys returns from lunch later in the day and just sits down at his desk when the phone rings. The warden's assistant on Alcatraz tells Keys that the guards want him to come out.

"What's happening?" Keys asks.

The warden's man on the phone says that the prisoner is ready to make any deal Keys wants.

With a broad grin on his face, Keys thanks the man and says he will be out as soon as possible. He leaves a message for Walsh. At an adjacent office Keys hauls an owlish looking man with thick glasses up from behind a desk piled high with a stack of paper. The bewildered man struggles to keep from being rushed out of the office.

"Come with me, man, I've got some important shorthand work for you. It'll do you good to get out of the office and into the bay air." The man pulls away from Keys to retrieve his coat and hat. He stuffs a notebook and pencils in his pockets, then dutifully follows the agent to the elevator.

The shorthand man is a better sailor than Seidel was. Today's bay water is very choppy, the air quite cool. High clouds wash out the sun making Alcatraz look very dreary. One of the guards in charge of Seidel is waiting at the dock. "We've cleaned him up some and put him in the waiting room for you."

"How'd you do it?" Keys asks.

"A little moanin' and groanin' while we walked up and down the hallway. Then Chuck starts moanin' and carryin' on like he's the ghost of a sailor. He rattled the other cell doors and screamed that he wanted to find the Nazi. I yelled out sayin' we had to get out of the dungeon 'cause a ghost was lookin' for Seidel.

"Chuck runs down the hall and hits the stairs hard. Seidel chimes in sayin' we can't leave him behind. We left him in the cell for a couple hours but he started cryin' a lot. I asked him if he was ready to talk to you and he said he'd do anything we wanted."

Seidel, manacled and unshaven, sits hunched over a desk. He looks haggard, years older, and meek. Keys pulls out a chair for the shorthand man and one for himself. He offers Seidel a cigarette, then puts the pack down close in front of him. "I want all the names of the people you have in the shipyards to start with."

Seidel looks up at Keys; there are dark circles under his eyes. "I don't know that I can remember all the names."

Keys slaps his hand down on the table. "Give me what I ask for now. If I leave here without everything I ask you for you'll rot in your dungeon cell. I will not come out here again; you have this one chance to help yourself. I don't know how many good American lives you're responsible for. I have no pity for you.

"The guards here don't even want to go back down to the dungeon with you. You've stirred up some bad things down there. I don't care; I'll take you back down there myself. Or you can stay up here in the comfort of A block while I verify what you tell me.

"If you don't lie to me, you'll go to federal court to answer for your crimes; I'll put in a good word for you. Start with the names. Then I need to know who you report to and how you get your information out."

It is well past midnight before Keys calls for a Coast Guard cutter to take him and the shorthand man back to San Francisco. Before Keys drops the man off he tells him to be ready to go back to Alcatraz the next day. He wants to get all the dope he can before Seidel gets his courage back.

The next morning Keys is at headquarters early. When Walsh comes in he finds Keys in a cheerful mood.

"You look like the cat that ate the canary."

"You're lookin' at a contented man, Jer. Those guards on Alcatraz scared the wits outta Seidel. He couldn't get the dope out fast enough. I almost feel sorry for the guy; he's aged a good ten years in two days. I'm headed back after lunch. I've got the boss' permission to use all hands to verify the dope we're getting.

"The people at the shipyards Seidel's been getting' information from are guys that he's either blackmailed or in some cases kidnapped or killed a family member. So far I only see a few cases where people are willing to sell out for money. I've got the legal department making out arrest warrants and I want you and a few men to start rounding up these people.

"We won this one, Jerry. I feel better than I have in years. This is what I signed up for. We need to get Seidel's fishmonger to send off the radar dope and we're pretty much done. That's how Seidel's been gettin' his dope out; the fishmonger takes it to Mexico in the bread van. The Nazi's are in Mexico with big money to bribe the Mexican government. They're operating down there with a free hand.

"I'm gonna have Seidel contact the fishmonger to take the drawing to the Nazi's in Mexico. We'll shadow the fishmonger and let him lead us to the spy ring there. When we can get a handle on who's who down there, we'll round all of 'em up after they get the radar dope out.

"When we wrap this up the party's on me. After I finish with Seidel I'll go see Devin. I'm sure he'll be happy this is over and he can get back to his war."

The next morning when Walsh gets to headquarters to report his progress at rounding up the people on his arrest list, he sees Keys is not as happy as yesterday.

"So what's up, Barry? You were on top of the world yesterday."

"Yeah, Jer, it's a rotten world out there sometimes. I gotta go tell Devin that the girl that got him into this is part of Seidel's gang. She was married to Dieter and the kid Nick was so worried about they got from an orphanage in New York. The kid's vanished. Seidel said Dieter was roughing the kid up and he took off. I've contacted the orphanage to get the kid's real name and history. I'm not at all sure we'll ever find him.

"Seidel swears the kid's not dead; he says the boy they called Benny packed his clothes, took some food and left. I guess younger kids have made it out on their own but it's gotta be tough. Anyway I owe it to Nick to tell him about it and to get Doris in custody."

Mare Island is as busy as ever; Keys dodges workers and sailors who are head-down hard at it. He knocks, then enters the small shack where the captain of the *Bullshark* coordinates the outfitting of his new boat. Captain Shaver stands up, wearing a frown, as Keys enters. Keys comes forward with his hand out.

"Shake hands, Captain, we've won this one."

Shaver wearily shakes Keys' hand. "Does this mean I've got Devin back?"

"Yes sir, Nick's free. I'd just like to thank him; we wouldn't have broken this one without him, or without your cooperation. This is a big deal, Captain. I can't go into specifics but a major spy ring is broken. Is Nick around? I won't keep him. I just want to say thanks."

"I'm happy it's over, Keys. I need his full attention. We're ready for sea trials next week. He's at building 229 putting together the manuals he wants. I would imagine he's on his way back by now. He usually walks back past the sub building ways. Just walk down the waterfront toward the dry docks and look for the tall steel gantries between the shipbuilding ways."

Keys walks down Waterfront Avenue; the sun, bright in the sky, warms his face. A pleasant day ruined by bearing bad news. The agent is wary of the information he's going to deliver. Devin was deceived into caring; Keys knows he will not take the news well.

At the ferry slip he turns to his right to make his way past Number 1 ways. The submarine under construction on this way has heavy wood scaffolding surrounding the sub reaching several stories skyward. Shipyard workers swarm over the boat, turning out yet another amazingly intricate war machine in just a few months.

Keys continues to Railroad Avenue and crosses to Alden Park where he looks around searching for Nick when he sees the sailor carrying a large cardboard box heading his way. "Hey sailor, how's it goin'?"

Nick looks up to see Keys headed toward him. "Hi, Barry. Look, I'm really busy, the captain's not gonna let me take more time away."

"I'm not here to take you away, Nick. We got Seidel to talk and we're wrapping the whole thing up. I'll walk with you back to your boat." Walking by Nick's side Keys looks at the sailor, then blurts out, "I came to tell you that Doris was in on the whole thing."

Nick stops walking. "What?"

Keys shrugs his shoulders. "Nick, she was married to Dieter. The whole thing was a scam to get you sucked in. The boy Benny is an orphan they picked up in New York; he's run away. We haven't been able to find her yet. I have an arrest warrant for her in my pocket."

Without a word Nick turns away. He turns between the old brick buildings 45 and 46 headed back to his boat. Keys hurries to catch up. The noise of construction on the submarine drowns out Keys' voice.

Nick feels something punch the box he's carrying in front of him. Looking around in confusion, Nick sees Doris step out from behind a gantry girder with a pistol pointed at him. Keys moves to Nick's side drawing his pistol.

Fearing Keys will have to shoot Doris, Nick shoves Keys away toward the scaffolding. Keys stumbles over an air hose, going down to the ground hard.

Doris screams hysterically, "I'm here to kill you. God damn you, I'm going to kill you. You ruined everything. You killed my husband, I hate you. I hate everything about you, I hate this place. I'm going to make you pay!"

Without hesitating Nick holds up the heavy box as a shield and runs toward Doris. She raises the pistol in both hands, trying to steady her aim. Nick is only yards away coming fast. She takes aim at Nick's head, drawing a bead on the face she hates. A heavy wood plank crashes to the ground in front of her and bounces up, almost hitting her.

Nick drops the box, sprints the last few yards, and knocks the gun from her hands. Doris screams in fury lashing out with her fists. Nick puts his arms around her to keep her from scratching his face. When she tries to knee him, he turns her around, pulling her arms down behind her.

Keys hobbles over to them, pulling handcuffs from his back pocket.

"She'd a killed you if that guy on the scaffolding hadn't thrown that plank. You've more guts than good sense, and you ruined another good pair of my pants. I've got a good mind to bill the damned Navy."

Doris, with her hands cuffed behind her, sinks to the ground wailing. Tears streak down her face as Keys pulls her to her feet.

"I'll kill you if it's the last thing I ever do," she threatens Nick.

"You'll never get the chance," Keys says.

A crowd of workers begin to gather around, anxious to see what all the excitement's about.

Keys holds on to Doris' manacles as he bends down to pick up her gun. Pulling the struggling woman away, he says over his shoulder, "I'll be seeing you, Nick; I've got to get this she-devil back to the city."

Nick, inspecting the bullet hole in the manuals that spilled out of the box, shouts at Keys' back, "Not if I see you first."

Chapter 29

At the Sutter Street FBI headquarters in San Francisco Keys meets with Walsh and three other agents to plan their next steps.

"I don't know that we'll get much out of Doris. We do know her real name is Freda Getman and that she and her father were Bund members in upstate New York. She met Dieter there and when the Bunds came under heavy federal scrutiny she and Dieter joined their cousin Willi here.

"The boy they took from an orphanage in New York ran away before Dieter was killed by Willi, so Seidel says. I have the state and local cops looking for him. Seidel notified the fishmonger to pick up the radar drawing and take it to Mexico. Jerry, take two men with you and get Willi out of lockup. Take him to the North Beach restaurant to hand over the drawing Washington sent.

"The Mexican fishmonger has to see Willi to make this work. He knows Willi. Jerry, you go in with Willi and make sure he doesn't try anything stupid. Have him introduce you to the fish guy as a new recruit to Seidel's gang. This has to go right. We've come too far to screw up now.

"I've briefed the boss and he's asked for a complete report on our investigation so far. He's gonna send the report to Washington and the big brass are to give us final instructions. Other than tailing Willi, you have all done an outstanding job. Learn from losing Nick in the bread van; I don't want to have that happen again. Okay, don't look so hang dog; you can be proud of breaking up an important spy ring.

"The last pieces of the puzzle are coming together, so don't get sloppy. I want to find out more about what we believe are communist spies that are operating in our own back yard. I'm gonna put together a plan to follow anyone who is interested in Nick Devin or the whereabouts of Clark or his pal Mikhail. We need to do this without stepping on Washington's toes.

"Don't forget I'm throwing a little celebration next Saturday night at John's Grill on Ellis."

Later in the day Keys finishes his report and takes it to his boss.

Keys enters the boss' office at the end of the hallway and lays the report on the man's cluttered desk.

Frank Gray, Keys' boss, always reminds Keys of a caged animal. Gray is a big man with very large hands. At rare times when Keys has shaken the man's hand, his own became lost in Gray's palm. Suits, though well-tailored, look too small, his top shirt collar button is usually unbuttoned, his tie pulled loose.

"Good job, Keys. Washington is anxious to read your report. I don't mind telling you that I'm a little peeved that the new agents who are buzzing around from D.C. don't share anything and report to directly to headquarters. Maybe this will show 'em we still know our business here.

"I'll read through it first, then fire it off. Whatever is going on in Berkeley is supposed to be a big secret.

So uncovering Communists in one of our investigations will, I think, be a revelation. Maybe they'll share some dope. It's not as though we don't know what kind of work Professor Lawrence does at Berkeley."

"Thanks, boss," Keys says. "I've got my team on the lookout for possible Communists interested in our investigations and we're following up on Seidel's Mexican connection."

Gray runs his finger around the inside of his shirt collar as if the unbuttoned collar is strangling him. "Solid work, Keys. Keep me posted."

Keys returns to his desk in a jubilant mood. He phones Mare Island in search of Nick Devin.

"Hello, Keys, what's cookin?" Nick has a finger in his ear to shut out the noise from the shipyard machine shop where he was called to the phone. "I hope you're callin' to say job well done and goodbye."

"Well, now, that's real nice; I thought we were pals," Keys replies. "As a matter of fact I called to invite you to a party I'm puttin' on to celebrate the end of this case. Captain Shaver told me you have one last weekend off before you ship out. That's how I found you to get you on the phone. I'm buyin'.""

"Well, in that case, who all's gonna be there, old pal? My parents are coming up if they can get off work."

"You're welcome to bring them along, Nick. Walsh is bringin' his girl, the guys from my crew that were at Seidel's are comin' and a couple a guards from Alcatraz are bringin' their wives."

"So you're the only single? You need to find yourself a good woman, you old goat," Nick provokes with a friendly jibe.

Keys' brow wrinkles. "You're getting on my nerves here, boy. I've got a good woman only she won't be there."

"Would that be Mary?" Nick asks.

"How the hell do you know anything about Mary?"

"Walsh and I were talkin' about stuff when he took me to the ferry. We were kinda hyped up after all the action was over and babbled on about you and him. He told me about him findin' you at a hospital after you ran into your first bullet, and it does seem to me that you are prone to finding lead. Anyway he said that your wife Mary left because she was afraid you'd get yourself killed.

"We had some time waitin' on the ferry, so we sat on the dock while the other guys watched Willi. He told me you sent him to check me out and that he met my parents. He had dinner with them, and they had a good time together. He liked my mom and dad and said he planned to look at some of the woodwork in the wineries that my granddad worked on. He's an easy guy to listen to."

"Yeah, he talks too much," Keys interjects. "Nice dependable guy but he talks too much."

"Don't tell him I ratted him out, Keys. He's a good man and loyal to you. I love a good tale and Walsh is almost as good as Navy guys at spinning a yarn. So where's this shindig takin' place?"

"I got the upstairs room at John's Grill on Ellis Street. It's a great party room and, if you didn't know, it was a Dashiell Hammett hangout. It's in one of his novels; I can't remember which one right now."

"Sounds like a plan; I've never been upstairs. Oh, and it was in *The Maltese Falcon*. Spade ordered chops. So what time's it start?"

Keys chuckles. "Yeah, yeah, that's right, oh learned one. Dinner's at six, eighteen hundred to you, next Saturday. It's over when we run 'em outta booze or we run outta wild tales of our daring adventures."

Keys leaves the building feeling good about the job. Night is closing in, foghorns moan in the distance. The air is clean with a hint of the sea. The agent strolls along Montgomery Street to Bush, then the five blocks to his apartment on Mason.

At home he turns up the steam heat in the living room before opening a beer to relax in a chair and read the evening Trib. Morning finds him still in the chair, his back stiff. The room is very warm from the heat he never turned down the night before.

Uncoiling from the chair to stretch, he heads for the bathroom, shedding his clothes on the way to the shower. Showered and shaved, Keys heads for a small restaurant on Bush for eggs and bacon to get him kick-started. Sunday traffic is light, making for an easy walk to headquarters.

On entering the office his boss Frank Gray is waiting by his desk. Keys immediately feels the lightness shift from his mood.

"I thought you'd be here earlier. Follow me into my office, Barry, we need to talk," Gray commands.

Keys thinks it's even worse than he thought.

"Come in and close the door after you," Gray orders.

"Have a seat. I'm not going to beat around the bush. We are ordered to stand down from any further investigations that could compromise Washington's agents currently involved in Berkeley and Mexico."

Keys, without thinking, blurts out, "What the hell does that mean?"

"Take it easy, Keys. This isn't my idea, and I don't take kindly to being yelled at."

"I'm sorry, sir. I didn't think before openin' my big mouth. I don't really care about Berkeley, but I need to be able to finish the Seidel case."

"Barry, my orders are that Washington will take over from here. Seidel's Mexican connection is strictly off limits to us. Let me make that perfectly clear. Mexican involvement with Germany and Japan is only to be investigated by agents designated by Washington. I was told this morning to rein in my mavericks."

Keys' shoulders hunch up. "Mavericks? They think my guys are wild cows?"

"They think you're the maverick," Gray says pointing his finger at Keys.

"The term was that you are known to go off the reservation, and that any maverick behavior by you will not be tolerated."

"Where does that come from, sir?"

"Come on, Barry, how many times have you butted into local police affairs? Not to mention the time you slapped the hell out of the Mexican Federale that you accused of running drugs. The Mexicans made a big stink over that. They sent their ambassador to Hoover for God's sake. That little affair must have slipped your mind."

"Christ, boss, we almost got that sailor killed. I got shot. That investigation is ours. Are they even gonna tell us if the Germans bought the radar scheme?"

"I'll let you know what I know when I get back from Washington; I'm flying out today. But I will personally wring your neck if you poke your nose in this any more. Do you understand what I'm saying here, Barry? I don't want any misunderstanding on this."

"Yes, sir, I understand. Do you have anything you want me to do?"

"We still have the black market thing going on here, and some Japanese aliens that are masquerading as Chinese. That should keep you busy until I get back. Barry, you did a good job. I don't like this any better than you do."

Keys gets up from the chair fuming. He turns to leave without another word.

From behind him Gray calls, "Don't slam the door, Keys."

Chapter 30

Keys tells Walsh they've been taken off the Seidel case. Walsh is as upset as Keys is.

"What the hell are they thinkin'?" Walsh angrily exclaims.

"That's just what I said. This stinks, but Gray says stay away or he's gonna wring my neck. So I want you to make sure that the guys you have shadowing the fishmonger report back when they get to the Mexican border. Make sure they know Washington is sending agents to take over. I don't want our guys to interfere with them.

"The boss is gone; he's flyin' back to D.C. so I'm takin' the rest of the day off. We're back on black market crap and fake Chinese. I'll see you tomorrow."

Keys walks blindly back to his apartment. Head down, hands in his pockets, the noise and traffic of the city go unnoticed. He tries to call Mary. The phone is answered by her roommates both times he calls, with the same, "She's not here."

Not wanting his imagination to run away with thoughts of what Mary could be doing, he heads out for an early dinner. Returning to the apartment after dinner, he listens to the news on the radio, reads the paper then decides the day is better left behind and heads off to bed.

The shrill ring of the phone wakes Keys from a restless sleep. Reaching out to pick up the receiver he squints at the bedside alarm clock to see the dim glow of the hands indicates 5 a.m. Frank Gray's voice growls in his ear.

"Wake up, Keys, and get to the office. The agents that were sent to tail the fishmonger haven't reported in. If you still have people there have them find out what happened. I want you to call me back as soon as possible with a report. Get to it, Barry, I'm wearin' a hole in the assistant director's carpet."

Keys dresses quickly and rushes to the office. He calls the hotel in El Centro where his agents are staying to issue orders.

"Find the Washington agents and tell me why they haven't reported in. I mean right now; they could be in trouble, the boss is waitin' in D.C. Call me back. Hubba-hubba."

Ignoring the harsh taste of cigarettes before his first coffee, he waits for his agents to report back. It's a three-cigarette wait before his phone rings. Keys takes a short message, then calls D.C.

"Give me Frank Gray in the assistant director's office," Keys bellows into his phone.

"Boss, our guys found the Washington agents out cold in their room. They were drugged. They came into El Centro talkin' big, actin' tough', flashin' their badges. There's no tellin' who slipped 'em a mickey. Our men are on the fishmonger, and he's on the move."

"I'll get right back to you, Keys," Gray replies.

Ten minutes later Keys listens to Frank Gray on the phone.

"Get to El Centro as soon as you can. You'll be the Agent-In-Charge. I'm on the next plane back to Sutter Street."

"Boss, I've heard back from our men. The fishmonger crossed the border and is headed down Route Five. San Felipe is the only place he can be going. If you'll authorize transport, I can be in San Felipe before he gets there. The Army has an airfield near their radar station just outside the village."

"I'll back whatever you need, but step lightly, Barry. We need the Germans to get the radar dope without them suspecting any involvement from us."

Jerry Walsh stands at the edge of Keys' desk. Keys raises his right hand, making the okay sign. He tells Gray that he will do his best and hangs up the phone.

"It's all ours, Jerry. The boss sounded pretty pleased too. I'll bet he won't rub it in though."

Walsh smiles, nodding his head. "I'll bet he won't either; that's why he's the boss."

Keys frowns, but without any real anger. "I might take exception to that only we've got too much work to do. You're gonna fly to El Centro on an Army Dakota. I want you to get a car and drive down to San Felipe so we'll have a car if we need it. Make sure the car's got no government markings.

I'm on a two-seater TP-51. We're both flying out of Hamilton. I'll take our pistols with me. The Mexican cops won't even let our soldiers cross the border with firearms.

"When you get to San Felipe you don't know me. I'm gonna go as a private dick looking for a girl that ran off with her boyfriend. My story will be that her family wants her back before she's soiled. You're down there

189

to fish. Ask around for a good boat to take you out. Get to know as many people as you can without them thinkin' you're askin' too many questions. We may need a good boat man.

"I'm pretty sure the fishmonger isn't going any farther than San Felipe. So that means he'll pass the dope in the village. We know the Germans have agents around Mexico City. If he passes the radar dope in San Felipe to German agents, they'll have to cross the Sea of Cortez to get back to Mexico City.

"With a car and a boat available to us, even if he doesn't pass the dope in San Felipe, we'll be able to follow him. Give me the name and a picture of the fishmonger guy."

Walsh returns from his desk with a photo.

"His name is Francisco Reyes, he's 45 and he's a real fishmonger. He's been sellin' fish here for ten years. Seidel bought him the van so Reyes would bring fish to his restaurant exclusively. Reyes also sells to restaurants in L.A. Seidel doesn't seem to care about that. I don't think he's a real bad guy; he just does what Seidel tells him to do. He may think he's passing orders for drugs or girls."

"Okay, it doesn't matter at this stage, Jerry. When you get to El Centro tell our guys on the ground there to fly to Mexico City. I want them to coordinate with our agent there and cover the German hangouts. If we miss the pass-off or can't tail our men, we may save the operation on the Mexico City end. Saddle up, we've got Army planes waiting."

Hamilton Field, nestled by the side of lush green hills north of San Francisco, feels like a beehive. Planes are taking off and landing. Huge hangers house

190

hundreds of aircraft. Ground personnel are shuttling over the expanse of shimmering white concrete going about the business of keeping America's military might in the air.

Keys stows a small bag of clothes, takes a brief course in parachuting and is strapped into the back seat of the TP-51. The pilot looks to Keys as if he should still be in high school. The man's attempt at a mustache does little to age his image.

Behind the controls of the 1500-horsepower machine the man immediately displays his no-nonsense confident ability. The plane rushes into the air with a force that flattens Keys against his seat back. This sensation of speed is enhanced by the bellow of the big V-12 engine. The pilot reminds Keys to strap on his oxygen mask as the 11-foot four-bladed propellers chew the air to snap them above 20,000 feet.

Keys enjoys the flight, watching the multi-colored patches of earth below stream by. To the east the white tips of the Sierra Nevadas are magnificent in the sunlight. He's surprised when the plane descends to a brown desert runway. The beautiful shimmering blue of the Sea of Cortez laps at the beach by the little village of San Felipe.

An Army jeep spewing a smoky dust trail pulls up to the plane. Keys climbs out pulling his small bag over the cockpit side. He slaps the side of the plane and yells over the engine noise and prop wash to the pilot. "That's an experience I won't soon forget. Thanks."

The pilot gives Keys an easy salute before busying with the radio.

"Where to?" asks the jeep driver.

"I need to find a place on the north side of the city where I can watch the road. A cold beer would be good too."

"Yes sir, it sure would."

"Okay soldier, I'm buyin'."

"Yes sir, I know just the place."

Seated at a rough wood table near the road coming into the village, Keys and the army corporal raise their bottles of cerveza. Off in the distance heat shimmers distort the contours of the land. Keys sees a flash of light through the shimmers, then another. Sunlight winks off a car windshield as the car jounces over the road's surface.

"I may need you to follow a car for me, Corporal. You think you can do that without being too obvious?"

"You mean like 'follow that car'? Yes sir, I'm your man."

Keys tips his bottle up to finish the beer as the car closes on them. As the car passes he stands to head for the jeep. Turning as the car goes by, he sees it is the fishmonger's black van that slows to a stop in front of a cantina not fifty yards from where he is. Keys recognizes Francisco Reyes getting out of the van carrying a brown briefcase.

"Okay, Corporal, I'll take from here. Thanks for the ride."

"Yes sir, if you need anything I'm Max Sanor and I'm just a beer away."

"Very good of you soldier, now get outta here, will you?"

Keys picks up his bag and heads for the cantina Reyes went into. Hustling to the cantina, Keys is anxious to see if Reyes passes the briefcase. He slows at the cantina door to take in the interior's layout and occupants. To his right is a long board resting on whiskey barrels. Rough talk snaps his head to the left. Farther into the adobe he sees a big man in ragged clothes tugging on Reyes' briefcase.

Keys steps to his left a few paces and bumps into the man accosting Reyes. The man turns with fire in his eyes. Keys raises both hands and says, "Sorry pal, I just stumbled."

"Gringo!" The man snarls, and lashes out with a huge fist.

Keys drops his bag and pulls his head back from the fist to slap the man's arm down. He closes his right hand into a fist and punches the man hard in the throat. The man goes down on his knees gasping, holding his throat. Keys picks up his bag, pulls the man to his feet and shoves him toward the entrance.

Reyes, clutching the briefcase to his chest, says, "Gracias señor."

Keys holds out his hand to shake. "You speak English? Maybe you can help me."

"What may I do for you, sir?" Reyes asks.

Keys takes a photo of a young girl from his pocket to show to Reyes. "I'm a private detective from Los Angeles. I'm looking for this girl for her family. She's run off with a boy and I believe they came through here headed to Mexico City. Could you ask the men here if they've seen her? I'll buy a beer for anyone with any information."

Reyes takes the photo. "I will show them the picture, and let me bring you a cerveza. José wanted me to buy him more; he thought I had money in this bag. I think there are only papers for the restaurant in this. My big boss sends me with this to give to his partners from Mexico City. He would be very angry if José took it from me."

Reyes shows the photo to the half dozen men in the room, then brings Keys an amber bottle of beer and one for himself.

"No one here has seen this girl. They are ashamed they did nothing to help me; most of them fear the temper of José when he drinks. Would you like to sit? I am to wait here for my boss' partners to deliver this bag."

"Thanks, keep the photo, I have more. Show it around if you would. I'll have to go on to Mexico City if I can't find her here. Is there a ship that goes there from San Felipe?"

"Yes," Reyes replies. "The next one will be here next week."

"That will be too late. I don't want to lose the girl; I don't know what plans they have after they reach Mexico City. How do the men you are waiting for get to the mainland?"

"They come in a seaplane that takes my fish to market in Puerto Vallarta. I do not think they will let you go with them. One of the partners is a sad, mean man; you would not like his company so much I think."

Keys drinks the beer savoring the taste. "I'll get going; I need to show the photo around and see if any one has seen the girl. I can't waste much time before I have to find a way to Mexico City. Thanks for your help, and the cerveza."

"De nada, señor."

Keys stays close to the cantina to watch for the hand off. Walking down the white sands of the beach,

Keys feels things have gone well. Gaining Reyes' trust was what he needed to be able to plan his next steps. He likes FBI work when he has an objective and is free to pursue it. The first cases he worked on after joining the bureau filled him pride to be a part of an elite force. He hopes that bringing this case to a successful conclusion will show Washington that he is still a man they can trust to get a job done.

The voices of men speaking in a foreign tongue shake him from his reverie. Two men are walking toward him. One of them has his shoes in one hand, his trouser cuffs rolled up letting the water frothing up the sand roll over his feet. The other man walks well away from the water, harshly mocking the barefoot man.

As the three men near each other, Keys tips his straw hat in greeting. The man in the surf tips his but his partner takes no notice. Closer to them now, Keys can see deep burn scars on the left side of the man's face who is farther away from the water. His skin along the jaw line sags as if some flames had melted his flesh. The scars make Keys think of pilots see has seen in burn wards. He looks at the man's left hand; the hand is curled and disfigured.

Keys veers off to his right toward the village before they pass each other. He shows the photo he has to anyone he can find to preserve his cover before quickly doubling back to the cantina. In an alley he stands in the shade outside a flyspecked window watching Reyes turn over the briefcase to the two men from the beach.

Confident he has his spies, Keys knows he has to find Walsh and get a plane to beat them to Mexico City.

Chapter 31

On the side of the road a mile north of the village Keys rests with his back against the remnants of a crumbling adobe wall. His eyelids are drooping when the now familiar flashes of sunlight wink off a windshield in the distance. Getting to his feet, Keys brushes off the back of his pants and stretches. He waves his arms as a surprised Walsh brings his car to a stop.

Keys picks up his bag and walks to the driver's door. "Slide over, Jer, I'll drive. I'll tell you the whole story on the way back to El Centro; we'll grab a plane there and head to Mexico City."

Jolted awake as the plane lands at Mexico City, Keys rubs his eyes to clear the sleep. The plane shudders to a stop with Keys and Walsh ready at the door to leave. When the ground crew bumps the roll-up stairway into the plane's exit, Keys is first man out. He grabs the handrail, feeling lightheaded. Walsh is right behind Keys.

"You alright, Barry?" Walsh asks.

"Yeah I'm okay, just felt lightheaded for a moment. That morning sun blinded me at the first step."

Walsh follows Keys down the stairs. "You know this place is over 7300 feet above sea level don't you?"

At the bottom of the stairs Keys fills his lungs with a deep breath. "I didn't remember until you said it. I feel better already. Where are our guys gonna pick us up?"

"I asked Ray Davis to pick us up. He said we've been assigned a local man who knows the city to help us."

At the car Davis takes their bags and puts them in the trunk of the four-door Pontiac.

Keys settles into the back seat. "Say, this is a nice car. Things must be good here; I'd like to have a car this nice back home."

"You ain't seen nothin' yet," Davis says. "Manny's got us at the ritziest hotel I've ever been to."

"Who's Manny?" Keys asks.

Davis looks into the back seat in rear view mirror. "He's the guy the local office sent us. He seems to know everyone and their brother."

"I hope you had a good time," Keys says. "But we won't be staying there. We're supposed to be low-key. I don't want anyone to take notice of us. I'm here posing as a private dick. Walsh is here as an accountant and you and Bill Cross are draft dodgers. Do any of those people sound like they'd be high-profile?"

"No, sir," Davis replies. "Bill and I there stayed last night, but we didn't go out. We were both too tired."

"Okay, probably no harm done. Where's Bill and this Manny now?"

"Bill's checking on flights coming in from Puerto Vallarta and Manny's probably at the Hotel Del Prado bar."

Keys looks at his watch. "Pretty early for that; is your stuff at this hotel?"

"Yes sir," Davis says.

"Okay, let's head there and pick up your things. We'll need to get to Bill so we can communicate. After we see Bill we'll find some outta-the-way hotel for Walsh and me. You get Bill's stuff and find some place near where we're gonna be."

When they stop in front of the elaborate art deco hotel, Keys tells Davis to get the luggage and have Manny meet them at the car. He doesn't want all of them seen together. Davis comes out of the hotel with two suitcases; a tall man follows. He is a young man dressed in an immaculate white suit with slicked back black hair, a neatly-trimmed mustache, and dark glasses.

Keys gets out of the car to shake hands with the home agent. The home agent ignores Keys' offered hand. "What is the meaning of this? I have made the arrangements; you will stay here."

"Manny, is it?" Keys asks. "You don't give the orders here, son, I do. We need to be low-key; I don't want to attract attention. Our job is to follow the Germans to wherever they go to pass the information, without them knowing we are on to them. Thanks for putting the guys up in style but we can't stay."

"You may go, bub," Manny sneers. "If you need my services, I will be here."

"Who do you report to?" Keys asks.

"I report only to the highest man in Mexico," Manny replies.

Walsh and Davis watch the back and forth. Keys is getting agitated. "Well, Manny," Keys says, "tell your boss that we won't be needing your services."

"My name is Manuel, not Manny. You are as crude as most of your kind."

Keys' face flushes. His fists clinch before he takes a breath and shoves his hands in his pockets. "Get outta here, Manuel. We're done here."

"Get outta here. You tell me get outta here," Manny says. "You insolent pig." He slaps Keys' face with an open hand.

Keys' fist comes out of his pocket in a flash. The force of Keys' punch to the jaw sends Manuel to the sidewalk, the dark glasses flying off his face. After a minute to clear his head, Manuel pushes himself up on his elbows; one hand comes up to work his jaw. "You will regret that, señor."

"You're gonna regret it a lot more, Manny, if you don't get your dandy boy ass outta here."

Manuel makes a show of getting up, taking a handkerchief from his pocket to dab his mouth. He dusts himself off with the handkerchief before picking up his dark glasses and walking back across the street to the Hotel Del Prado.

"He's gotta be connected to a high-ranked man at the local office. Maybe somebody's son or worse," Walsh speculates. "I hope he doesn't make anymore trouble for us. Don't get pissed Barry; I don't blame you, and I'll tell that to anybody that'll listen too."

Davis, uncomfortable with the altercation, tries to go unnoticed.

"Thanks, Jer, let's get back to Bill quick. If he's on to something he won't know where to find us."

Davis drives the Pontiac with Keys and Walsh to the airport. Keys instructs Davis from the back seat of the car.

"Have Cross come out here to the car to report. I'll take the next watch in the airport. Jerry, take the guys and go find some small hotels somewhere close and page me here with their phone numbers."

Cross comes out with Davis to report that the next flight from Puerto Vallarta should be landing in two hours.

Keys gets out of the car, he leans on the door sill, speaking into the car. "Okay, that should give you all time to get settled. Jerry, I want everybody here in an hour and a half. You go rent a car and take Davis with you. I'll take Cross and we'll double team the Germans. These guys aren't dumb; they've operated here even after we busted the Georg Nicolaus spy ring.

"We just need to see if they'll lead us to the rest of their rats. If we get spotted we'll lose 'em. Try to get photos of anyone they come in contact with. You can be camera bug tourists but if they spot you fade quick; don't take anymore pictures of them. Here's your copy of the best street map I could find.

"If they split up Cross and I will take the scarred-face man. Jerry, you and Davis are on the other man. Watch for other tails; these guys may have others watching them. They could have their own guys making sure they're okay or any number of other agencies could be watching them. This city is full of spies. Be careful and we can tie this up and be back home in a day or two."

Keys enters the airport terminal building to get the lay of the land. Finding the arrival board he notes the time of the Puerto Vallarta flight. Wanting to see if anyone else is interested in the Germans, he goes to the information desk to show the photo of the young girl. After finding a man at the desk who speaks English, Keys explains with a voice that carries that he is a private detective looking for the girl in the photo.

The man behind the desk shakes is head negatively. Keys shows the photo to others in the terminal with the same outcome. Having established himself as a man with a mission he settles into a seat to wait for the flight while taking note of the faces he sees.

Keys goes to the phone booth when he is paged and talks to Walsh. He tells him to wait outside and have Davis ready to pick him up when he comes out of the terminal.

When the flight arrives the Germans are in the middle of the small group of arrivals. They are not met by anyone and as they wait for their baggage Keys goes outside. Davis pulls the Pontiac to the curb and Keys gets in.

"Drive past the cabs and pull into the parking lot. We'll wait and see if they get picked up or take a cab."

When the Germans come out of the terminal building to hail a cab, Keys is in position to take photos of both men with his prized Kodak EKTRA. Keys places the camera on the dash board of the Pontiac.

"Kill the engine," he says to Davis. "I don't want them to see me taking photos with the camera. The car needs to be still."

Without holding the camera up to his face Keys frames the photos, then clicks the shutter. The scarred-face German scans the area before ducking into the taxi. His scan passes by the Pontiac without hesitation.

Keys takes his camera from the dash. "Let 'em get a good headstart before you pull out."

The cab with the German spies leaves the airport heading west on a main multi-lane thoroughfare. Davis stays four or five cars back with Keys directing the tail. For a few miles traffic is light; closer to the center of Mexico City the traffic becomes congested. The cab they are tailing is in the right-hand lane and has to slow behind a bus; Keys tells Davis to pass the cab. Walsh takes up the tail several cars behind the cab.

Traffic is now heavy with cars, trucks, buses, and pedestrians all jostling for position, choking the street. Keys reaches outside the passenger window to adjust the side mirror so he can see the cab after it pulls around the bus.

"Keep your eyes on the road ahead, Davis; I'll watch the cab and tell you what to do."

Walsh closes on the cab as two cars turn off in front of him. He wants to pull back but is hemmed in. At a traffic signal he hesitates. When the cab goes through the signal two cars pull in ahead of him behind the cab. They go for several miles in stop-and-go traffic. Ahead Walsh sees a traffic cop standing on a platform in the middle of an intersection, his arm outstretched directing traffic.

The cop lowers his arm to turn to another direction. A car darts into the intersection and is hit by a streetcar. The cab with the Germans squirts through a gap behind the crumpled car before traffic is snarled. Walsh bashes the dashboard. "No, no, no," he yells.

Keys notes the carnage behind them, then sees the cab squirt through. Going with the flow of traffic, Davis passes by another intersection when Keys startles him.

"Turn right, they turned behind us. Get goin'! Walsh is trapped; turn right and stand on the gas."

Davis turns and powers down the street. At the next intersection, Keys orders Davis to turn again. Davis turns right, romps down on the throttle, tires squealing.

The cab just passes them at the intersection. Davis turns left to follow. "Nice work, Davis," Keys compliments. "That Indy car racer Jack Novac woulda been proud of the way you hit the gas. Don't get too close, traffic is getting lighter." Davis eases his grip on the steering wheel and lets out a breath.

The cab turns right past a park and stops. The two Germans get out with their bags and wait for a break in traffic before crossing the street.

"Let me out here," Keys barks. "The Germans are going over to a restaurant across the street. Go on around the block and look out for Walsh. If you don't see him, circle around again. I'll signal you when I want to be picked up. Walsh will meet us back at the hotel if he doesn't find us.

Keys throws his hat and coat into the car when he gets out and slings his camera's strap over his shoulder. Heading into the park he finds a vantage point behind a large statue of a man on a rearing horse. The two Germans meet a white-haired man at a sidewalk table in front of the restaurant.

The scarred-face man hands the man at the table an envelope before he sits down. Keys fires off a series of photos capturing the scene. He walks to another side of the park away of the restaurant to wait for Davis. Keys signals as the Pontiac comes into his view. When he gets into the car Davis says that Walsh is behind them.

"Go to the end of this block and stop," Keys tells Davis. "I want to talk to Walsh."

Walsh pulls in behind Davis as Keys gets out of the Pontiac.

Walsh shrugs when Keys comes to the car. "I'm sorry, man. There was no way to follow that cab."

"Don't worry, we've got 'em. I want you to follow the white-haired guy sitting with them at the table. The scarred-face man passed him an envelope and they all grinned at each other like it was Christmas. I'm gonna go report to our office here and see if they have any photos of the white-haired man; I've seen him someplace.

"Don't lose the guy, Jerry. I hope he's the last link. Call in when you can; I'll be at the local office or in our hotel waiting to hear from you. Be careful, I have a feeling white hair is plenty sharp; he may be the big cheese."

Chapter 32

Keys has Davis and Cross take him to the FBI office, leaving the other car for Walsh to use if he needs it. At the office Keys sends his two agents back to their hotel telling them he will call when he needs them. He knows he's made an enemy of Manuel Gamma but is unsure of what influence the man has or how it might affect Davis and Cross. He may need the two agents free and out of trouble.

As he signs in at the front desk he is told that the head agent wants to see him. The head man's office is at the end of a room furnished with several desks and a wall of file cabinets. Keys stops at the open door to knock on the door frame. There are two large framed pictures on the wall behind the desk. One is President Roosevelt; the other is J. Edgar Hoover.

The man at the desk has his head down reading the contents of a file folder. The top of his head is hairless. The skin is shiny showing a crease in his skull on the right side. He looks up, pulling the reading glasses from his weathered face and grins.

"Keys, you old son of a bitch. Still makin' trouble wherever you go, I see."

"Jim, I didn't know you were here. Who the hell would put you in charge of anything?"

James Spadman comes around his desk to give Keys a crushing hand shake. After he thumps Keys on the back he points to a chair. "Take a seat, troublemaker. If you're here to give me any grief, I'll give you that boxing lesson I should have finished in 'Frisco."

Keys raises both hands in surrender. "Not me, Jim. I can't tell you how happy I am to see you. I hope this is a good post for you. You deserve a good one after the beating you took from those strikers. I thought you retired."

"Retirement's for old fogies, Keys. I'm still in my prime. I've got more work here than you can shake a stick at. Spies around here are thicker than flies on cow crap. Washington says you're the man in charge of the secret drawing so, what can I do for you?"

"I need to report to you and to my home office. I've tailed the Germans from San Felipe to here. They just passed an envelope that I'm sure is the drawing to a white-haired guy I think I've seen before."

Spadman picks a folder up from his desk. "This guy would be kinda short with a white mustache that curls around to his sideburns?"

"That's the man. Who is he?" Keys asks.

"He's the guy we missed at the German consulate in Frisco in '41. He'd lammed out before we could arrest him."

Keys slaps the arm of his chair. "Damn! You're right. I must be getting old. I knew I'd seen that mug before."

"He's up in the world now, Keys; he's the big man here. If that drawing is the big deal Washington thinks it is, he'll be on a plane to Lisbon with it."

"That's perfect, that's just what we want. That'll wrap it up for us, Jim. How about dinner tonight?"

Spadman points to a battered suitcase. "Wish I could; I'm on my way up north to Monterrey. We don't arrest these German spies much anymore, we just feed 'em disinformation. I've got two spy guys up there that are trying to blackmail Mexican oil company executives who are supplying our war effort. I was on my way when I heard you were here.

"I want to give you the word on Manny Gamma. He's made out a complaint, saying you beat him up after he told you not to insult him."

"Jim, let me tell you…"

Spadman raises his hand. "Wait up, Keys. The guy's got some connection to the Federales that Washington thinks is important. He's too…"

Keys grins. "You mean dandy?"

"I don't think so, Keys. That's an act for his undercover work. The problem is he does what he wants, he doesn't listen, doesn't think he has to listen. For the rest of us that's no good but we're stuck with him. My advice is to stay away from him until you go home. I'll put in a good word for you."

"Okay, Jim. I wish we had more time. I'll send you a written report when I get back."

Keys shakes the head agent's hand across his desk. "Take care, Jim. You don't need another dent in your head."

Spadman absently runs his hand over the crease on his head. "You've got that right, Barry; you take care, too. Call me when you get back to 'Frisco. We can lie about old times."

Keys stops to read a message the man at the front desk gives him on his way out. Someone claiming to be an FBI informant wants to meet with Keys at an industrial complex on the western side of the city. The informant states that he has information vital to Keys' mission.

"Who gave you this message?" Keys asks the front desk man.

"I didn't see anyone sir. It was on the desk when I came back from a trip to the bathroom."

"Where's a phone I can use?" Keys asks.

Davis answers the phone in his hotel room. Keys asks if Walsh has called in. "He's here with us sir. We're just thinking about getting something to eat."

"Put him on, will you, Davis?"

"Hi, Barry, the white-haired guy went right to the airport. I recognized the street from when we came in and figured that's where he was headed. I stayed well back and waited 'til he was on the plane to get the flight information. He's booked on a flight to Caracas and on to Lisbon. I came back here to wait for you."

"Good job, Jer. I think that wraps it up for us and we can head back home. I've a message from someone who says he's an informant and he wants to meet me. I don't like it; I want you to back me up. Take down this address and meet me there."

Keys takes a cab to the address on the message and waits for Walsh. Night is closing in; there are few lights on and no one is about. A voice booms out of the darkness. "Hola, you Keys?"

"Yeah, I'm Keys. What do you want?"

A man moves into a circle of light cast by a streetlamp. He grins widely, highlighting a gold front tooth in the light. He takes a long bladed knife from his belt.

"I want you, señor."

Keys hears a scrape behind him. "I see you brought a friend. I take it you two were sent by Manny. You guys dandy boys, too?"

"You will die here; I will take pleasure to kill you, gringo."

Gold-tooth nods to his confederate to move in on Keys.

Keys lets his camera bag slip to the ground to pull his pistol.

"Pistola, pistola," the man behind Keys yells.

"You are not to have pistolas here," Gold-tooth says.

"I don't go anywhere without it," Keys replies. "I keep it with me for occasions just like this."

"You would be in much trouble to use the pistola; only Federales have pistolas."

"Amigo, everybody here has a gun. You must be too poor to own one. Put up your knives and go away. I'll let you live to pester someone else. You can tell Manny to come for me himself."

"I no get paid to run away. I don't think you can shoot dos."

Keys shows his teeth in a wide grin. "I don't need to shoot both of you. I'm gonna kill you and your friend's gonna run away.

"He will no run."

"Okay, amigo. He takes one more step and you're a dead man. If your friend doesn't run, he'll be dead too."

Keys raises his pistol, extending his arm to point the gun at the gold-toothed man.

Gold-tooth crouches slightly, turning his body to make his silhouette smaller. "Police pistolas don't shoot so good I think. Maybe you miss; maybe you no good shooter."

"You don't know anything about pistols, do you compadre? This is no police pistol. You'd know that if you knew guns." Keys rotates his wrist to show the pistol's frame.

"See, this is a .357 magnum. I load it with lead hollow-point bullets. I'm gonna aim for your gold tooth and the bullet is gonna take your whole head off. Your neck'll spout blood like a fountain 'cause your black heart won't have time to stop pumpin'. Your friend is then gonna run like a rabbit."

Keys turns the gun back on the gold-toothed man, slowly thumbing back the hammer, making a sharp click at each of the hammer's detents. He sees Gold-tooth's grin disappear; a tremor reflects on the blade of Gold-tooth's knife.

"I'm getting' tired of this, Goldie; let's see how brave you are. Go ahead, tell your man to take one more step. You'll never live to see him take another."

Headlights splash over the men; each of them raises a hand to shield his eyes. Tires squeal, the car slows, then turns toward the men. The brilliant headlight beams freeze the three men still as stone statues.

Gun drawn, Walsh rushes out of his car on the run.

"You are no worth this trouble, gringo. Manuel, he will have to kill you."

Both Gold-tooth and his friend shrink out of the lights and into the darkness.

"You okay, Barry?"

"Yeah, I'm good. Where the hell've you been?"

"I got lost, man; that map you gave me ain't the easiest thing to read, you know. It's dark and I gotta stop every so often to find the streets."

"It's okay, Jer, you timed it perfect anyway. Our friend Manny hired those boys to do me in. Let's get back to the hotel. I'm bushed. Tomorrow we'll pack up and get the hell outta here."

"Let's go find Manny first," Walsh angrily exclaims.

"No! If we did find him one of us is gonna get hurt. The boss tells me Washington thinks I'm a loose cannon as it is. I don't want to get stuck here tryin' to explain how I could let it happen. I'll put it in my report; the brass can deal with it. If they don't like it, I got my twenty years in."

Chapter 33

After working on their reports, Keys and Walsh snatch some sleep on the plane back to California. The two younger agents fidget trying to nap on the long flight. Landing at Hamilton Field, Walsh and Keys are first out of the plane, greeted by a pelting rain. Running for cover, they wait for Davis and Cross to emerge.

All four men are soaked by the time they reach Keys' car. The windshield wipers slap hard, fighting to clear enough water to see the road to San Francisco. Hidden puddles at the bottom of the hills in Marin are several inches deep. Each one sends up huge sheets of water from under the tires, threatening to pitch the car out of control. Keys battles the steering, then slows trying to keep the car from aquaplaning off the road.

White-knuckling the dangerous rain-slick road, they slither down the S-curved hill out of the Waldo Tunnel. The Golden Gate Bridge's towers disappear in thick fog. Keys drives under the low ceiling of fog, happy to be back in the city. Out of the parking garage the men perch their travel bags over their heads and sprint for the Hunter-Dulin Building. Before they get settled behind their desks, Frank Gray emerges from his office.

Without preamble he brusquely orders, "I want full typed reports on my desk before any of you leave today." Turning to Keys' desk he grumbles, "Keys, in my office."

Keys gets up from his desk; he and Walsh trade a look. Shaking his head with disgust, Keys follows Gray to his office.

Gray sits behind his desk and tells Keys to shut the door and sit.

"I'll take it standing," Keys says.

"Always your way, isn't it, Keys? You know what this is about, right?"

"From the way you just issued orders without telling the boys what a fine job we all did, I take you're pissed about something. So like I said, I'll take it standing."

"Washington just hauled my ass over the coals is what this is about, Keys. Their man in Mexico City says you beat him up when he found out you were selling guns down there."

Keys laughs. "That's a hot one. The guy in question, Manuel Gamma, tried to screw up our operation from the beginning. I told him to butt out and he smacked me. I slugged him, knocking him to the ground. This was all in front of Walsh, Davis, and Cross.

"After I reported to Jim Spadman I got a message to meet an informant on the west side of the city. When I got there two locals popped outta the dark and told me Manny sent them to kill me. If it hadn't been for Walsh getting there to save the day I'd of had to shoot both of them."

Gray watches Keys face as he tells his story. "So you're saying Washington's star Mexico City agent set out to ruin the operation and then to kill you. How do you know the two men were sent by Gamma?"

"A man with a gold tooth and a big knife said Gamma was going to pay him for killing me."

"Did Walsh witness that?"

"No, sir, he did not. You're tellin' me my word's not good enough for you anymore?"

Gray stands. "I'm telling you you're suspended until an investigation is completed in this matter. I have to take all of your reports back to Washington tonight. You were on top again, Keys. You blew it. Put your report on my desk when you finish it. I have to get the red-eye back to D.C."

"I finished my report on the plane. It's on my desk."

Keys turns to leave, walking to the door.

Gray shouts, "Don't…"

Keys slams the door hard. The pebbled glass panel in the door shatters; shards scatter like birdshot.

Keys walks quickly back through the office to snap up his bags on his way out. Walsh and the other men in the room look at Keys wide-eyed.

Keys pauses at the door. "Always wanted to do that. See you boys at John's Grill, don't be late."

Gray gingerly walks into the room over the shards of glass. Hands on hips he scans the desks. At Keys' desk Gray picks up the sheets of Keys' Mexico report. To no one in particular he says, "Damn good thing he's gone. I'd like to flatten his face an inch or two. Couple of you men get a broom and clean up that glass. Walsh, get a steno to type up this report."

Confined in the elevator, Keys' anger begins to melt. A brief grin comes to his face thinking of the

214

glass shattering before it disappears. "And that's why you ain't the boss," Keys mutters, mimicking Walsh.

A woman in the elevator, startled by Keys, looks up before looking away; she focuses intently on the floor-counting lights. When the golden doors open the woman is away in a flash. Keys continues to the ground floor, no longer pleased with himself.

Soaked to the skin by the time he gets home, Keys strips and heads for the shower. Under needles of hot water, Keys releases from his self-admonishment. A glimmer of doing something new comes to his mind. He needs something to bring back the passion, that sense of adventure. Toweling off, he thinks of Mary. Throwing on a terry robe, he goes to the phone.

Mary is not in and her roommates have no information to impart. Keys puts down the phone and goes to the refrigerator for a beer. Opening the refrigerator's door his nose wrinkles at the odor of spoiled milk and green mold on cheese. Cracking some ice, Keys takes a tall glass from a cabinet, a bottle of Scotch from another and pours three fingers.

Keys gets up several times during the night. He tries to read a book on criminal justice from the Main Library until the words become meaningless. Finally some light filters through the curtains and he hears sounds of traffic on Bush Street.

Keys dresses and goes out for breakfast. Deciding to walk, he pulls up the collar of his overcoat against the cool light drizzle. After breakfast Keys walks to Union Square puzzling on his future. He takes a turn around the square before deciding to walk down to The Embarcadero.

After watching the busy bay front, Keys heads out again.

Head down, hands in his pockets, Keys makes his way down a bustling Market Street almost a mile to John's Grill on Ellis. He has a beer at the bar, makes sure they are ready for the party upstairs and leaves. He buys some groceries on his way back to his apartment.

Having burned the morning without coming to a firm decision about the future, he sits in a chair by his bay window to watch traffic. Mary, he knows, is the key. He wonders if he could just forget her. He wonders if he is punishing himself by continuing to love her. He seldom calls her, not wanting to invade her privacy.

Mary does call occasionally, professing her love for him and at the same time praising her new life without him. Keys shakes his head as if to clear his mind. Tomorrow he will go to Marin and confront Mary. He has not in the past, he realizes, because he was afraid she could end their life together. He is not a man of indecision; tomorrow he'll have an answer.

Keys takes a nap and, after a shower, he calls Mary's rooming house. The woman on the phone seems to take some pleasure in telling Keys that Mary has left on a date with a handsome young sailor.

Maybe that's the end of the query, Keys thinks. A night of drinking and swapping stories will be his answer for tonight. Tomorrow is soon enough to be sad. He dresses and walks down Powell toward the glowing neon sign advertising John's Grill.

Walsh, Davis, and Cross are at the bar when Keys comes into the restaurant. Keys sweeps his hand toward the stairs. "Shall we adjourn to the upstairs, gentlemen?"

216

At the bar upstairs Walsh waits for Keys to take his first sip of his Scotch Mist before slapping his back.

"You shoulda seen Gray's face when he crunched through the glass. He was red as a beet. He said he'd like to flatten your face some. He made us retype our reports. All of us said we knew Gamma tried to have you killed. So what set you off? I loved the glass shattering, but what's the deal?"

Keys picks up his drink for another sip. "The thing that really frosted my ass was Gray tellin' me I was on top again before I screwed up the whole op. We all did damn fine work. We busted the whole set-up wide open. If Washington gets their heads out, Seidel could continue to send Germany all sorts of bad dope.

"I know I called this party, but I'm not in the best of moods."

Walsh clinks his glass with Keys. "Well, don't dwell on it; let's have a good time. It's going to be a good night."

Keys drains his glass. "It will be after a few more of these."

"Don't go sailor on us, Keys. You've got people here who respect you. Our guys deserve some reward for a job well done, too. God knows they didn't get it from Gray."

"Yeah sure, Jer. Where is our sailor boy, the hero, anyway?"

"He'll be here, Barry. I talked to him yesterday. You mad at him for something?"

"No, maybe I'm just mad at the world tonight. I'll get over it. As soon as he gets here we'll introduce everyone and have dinner."

Keys puts his Scotch down to go around the room and greet his guests. The two guards from Alcatraz are entertaining everyone with their stories of ghosts and goblins from the spooky depths of the prison. Keys' black mood begins to lighten. He returns to the bar asking for a club soda with lemon and lots of ice.

Voices are getting louder, pretty much in proportion with the amount of liquor consumed. Keys asks Walsh if they shouldn't get dinner served.

"Let's give him a half hour, Barry."

"Okay, I'm gonna tell the bartender to go easy on the booze 'til after we eat. I know Devin told you he'd be here. He's not the kinda guy to show up late."

"You worry too much, Barry; he'll show."

Keys listens to the Alcatraz guards tell a story about an attempted prison break. The two guards interrupt each other's narrative with different slants on the story. Keys and the other listeners are bowled over with what seems to be a practiced comedy act.

Keys turns away from the act when tapped on the back. Nick Devin stands arm in arm with Keys' wife Mary, wearing a grin from ear to ear.

"Hiya, Keys. Meet my date for the evening. She decided to leave ancient history for the excitement of a man with unparalleled energies."

Keys sees only Mary's thousand-watt smile. He stammers, "What?"

Mary uncoils from Devin and takes Keys by the arm. They walk across the room toward the windows overlooking Ellis Street. Keys is so overwhelmed he doesn't know whether to be shocked with indignation or delighted to see her.

Mary reaches for Keys' hand. She takes his hand in hers and looks into his eyes. "I love you, Barry Keys. I will not ever leave you again. I'm so sorry I was so selfish. I just couldn't stand the thought of you being killed. I understand now that was foolish. Men and women are dying everyday in this war. The whole world has gone mad. The love you and I share is the most rock-solid thing this world has to offer."

The tension within him melts as they look deep into each others eyes. Keys takes Mary in his arms and kisses her lips with a passion he feared was dead. The loud talk in the room stops, replaced by wild hoots, whistles, and applause. Keys looks up to see beaming faces full of good cheer. Mary smiles up at Keys, seeing his face flushed in a moment of unaccustomed embarrassment.

Nick comes forward to grab Keys' hand in a hearty handshake. He pulls Keys aside. "Barry, I want you to know I'm really happy for you, man. I don't want to rain on your parade, but before this party gets any crazier I'd like to know what's gonna happen to Doris. Do you think you'll ever find Benny?"

Keys has to take a moment to will himself back to an ugly scene. Mary watches each man's face as they talk. Her concern rises as she sees the light that was just in her husband's eyes fade. Keys now seems far away from her. He speaks to the sailor in a low voice. "On the trip back from Mare, she sat quietly without a word. When we got in the elevator on Sutter, she went nuts. With her hands cuffed behind her she tried to kick me; when I tried to calm her down, she bit me. I put her in a room to settle down and got a matron to sit with her.

"I came back to the room with some coffee. When I opened the door, the matron was standing over Doris' chair. She slapped her hard. I put the coffee down and yelled at the matron to stop. The woman backed away from Doris and looked at me with wild eyes. The matron said no one had ever said such vile things to her in her life. She made a beeline for the door. I'm tellin' you this because the slap seemed to bring Doris' mind back in focus.

"I asked if she was ready to make a statement. I won't mention the words she spit back at me. I sat down across from her at the table and thought of some way I could get her to talk. Finally I just told her what the penalty for treason is. I said if she would tell me she was forced to help the spies and give me the names of all the people she knew were involved, I could make things easier on her. I just wasn't getting through to her. I asked if she knew where Benny might have gone when he ran away. She just started crying, Nick. I really don't know if she was crying for Benny or for herself. She never said a word to me after that.

"My boss and the federal prosecutors want her to go on trial with the death penalty on the table. If she isn't hanged, she'll most like spend the rest of her life in prison. I have all of our offices nationwide looking for Benny. I don't have much hope we'll find him."

The lull in the man's conversation presents Mary with an opportunity to tug Keys away. The rest of the group, who had been wary of breaking up Nick's and Keys' serious conversation, gather around the couple to wish them well.

Chapter 34

They could hardly wait for the party to end. Taking a cab back to the apartment they made love as soon as they arrived. Keys felt as if he were just married again; they talked long into the morning. Mary wants to move back in with Keys and find a job in the city. Marinships overflows with workers now, but housing is severely limited. Leaving the job will provide someone with a place to live.

Keys gets up to go to the bathroom. Returning to bed, he steals back into the bedroom feeling like a school boy. In the morning light he watches Mary sleep. Her lovely face, framed by long beautiful auburn hair, stirs his soul. He watches her chest rise and fall thinking how contented and at peace she looks. He realizes he is content, he is at peace. Mary brought him the greatest gift one can give.

Mary wakes later in the morning to the smell of bacon. They sit at the little kitchen table eating breakfast and talking of the future. Keys tells Mary he is ready to quit the bureau. He feels he has established enough contacts in the area to open his own practice. Monday morning he wants to apply for a private investigator's license.

"What do you think? I don't have to take dangerous cases; I can take what I want."

221

Mary flutters her lashes. "Maybe I should be your Effie Perine."

Keys laughs. "Sam Spade's secretary? Sure, why not? We'll go look for an office and have some cards printed."

"Barry, we left so fast I didn't get a chance to say thank you to Nick."

"How did you two cook up that grand entrance, anyway?" Keys asks.

"Jerry Walsh called me a few weeks ago. I had made up my mind to come back to you but I couldn't leave Marinships then. I told Jerry nothing was settled. My boss said I could go but she wanted me to train my replacement. Jerry called again and said Nick wanted to bring me to your party as a surprise.

"I had to rush the training to get my ducks in a row. My clothes and things are still in boxes at the rooming house. We need to go pick them up. Oh, sorry, I got off track. Nick was bringing his parents to the train station so he picked me up and we all went to the station together. His father works at Douglas and had to be back today.

"Nick's parents are nice people. They didn't want to leave and his mother kept asking Nick to stay 'til their train left. That's why we were late to your party. I think Nick really wanted to do something nice for you. He said you'd make a hell of a submariner."

Keys clears dishes from the table; he kisses Mary on her forehead on his way to the sink. "The rain's let up, so let's go pick up your stuff. We'll go on over to Mare Island and say goodbye to Nick. He's a good guy. I think I might even miss him some."

Dark clouds glide across the sky north of the Golden Gate bringing short showers and patches of sunshine. The road shines with the wetness. Keys is relieved there are no flooded valleys, his car feels secure as he powers up the hill to Marinships' employee housing. Mary directs Keys to her building where they transfer her belongings to the car.

She introduces Keys to Thelma, one of the women living in the house. When they finish moving Mary gives the woman a hug and turns toward the car.

"You shoulda stayed with the sailor honey," the woman calls.

Mary turns back and winks. "Experience is the thing here, Thelma, if you know what I mean."

"Yeah," Thelma retorts. "But the sailor's got the looks and the stamina. If you know what I mean."

They both laugh. Mary puts her last bag in the car with Keys behind the wheel waiting.

"I'll bet that was the woman I talked to the other day."

"You mean the woman that told you I was out on a date with a young sailor?" Mary asks.

"Yep," Keys says.

"I'll bet you're right. Thelma's a card."

Keys doesn't reply. He heads north to Sears Point Road, the two lane road leading to Mare Island. At the guard shack Keys shows his FBI I.D. and Mary's Marinship card. They find a place to park off Railroad Avenue and walk to the waterfront by the old coal storage bunkers where the *Bullshark* is tied up.

Keys and Mary watch men carry cases of frozen food to the deck. They pass them to the hatch behind the fairwater from which they are loaded in cold storage aboard the boat. Nick Devin stands by the gangplank talking with another sailor.

"Hey Nick," Keys yells.

Nick winces, says something to the sailor and walks over to shake hands with Keys. "Hey Keys, how's it goin'? Hi Mary, good to see you."

Mary gives Nick a hug, then a kiss on the cheek. Whistles come from the sailors on the *Bullshark*.

Mary pulls back from Nick her face coloring. "I didn't mean to cause a commotion," she says.

Nick looks from Keys to Mary and grins. "Not at all. That'll be the scuttlebutt of the day. My rating with the crew probably just jumped 50 percent."

Keys, smiling, slaps Nick on the shoulder. "Stay away from my wife, you heel. It's a good thing you're leaving soon. I'm just joking, Nick. But how long before you go?"

"You that anxious to be rid of me, Keys?"

"No, Mary and I want to be on the Golden Gate Bridge when your boat leaves to see you off. We both want to wish you and your crew good hunting and a safe trip. You did a great job for us Nick. The FBI and I are grateful."

"I wanted to thank you for being so nice and for meeting your parents," Mary says. "I'll write to you and to your parents too. Do you get a chance to write when you're on patrol?"

"I write Mom and Dad all the time. I'd be happy to write to you, too. There are times writing is the best way to pass the time. Getting letters from home is always a treat. Reading how things are at home makes me think of all the good things we're fighting for.

"I love what the papers are calling the silent service, but I'd like the war to end soon. Well, it's good to see you both, I've got to get back onboard and make sure these monkeys get their work done."

After they trade addresses, Keys reaches out to shake Nick's hand. "If you get back this way you're always welcome at our house."

Nick takes Mary's hand; he kisses it smiling up at Keys. "She's too good for you, you old goat. See you later."

He walks away without looking back. Nick goes over the gangplank and starts to climb down a forward hatch. He stops, looks at Keys and Mary, gives them a very smart salute, then disappears down into the boat.

Mary turns to Keys with tears in her eyes. "I hope he comes back. I don't want to think about something terrible happening to him. He's such a nice boy. His parents are such good people. I hate this war."

Keys puts his arm around Mary's shoulders, feeling sorrow for her pain. "Nick told me he has the best boat from the best shipyard in the Navy. He's looking forward to taking the fight to the enemy. He said there's rarely a dry eye when they go past the carnage to enter or leave Pearl Harbor. Every man in the Navy wants to make Japan pay for our sailors who died that day."

Mary has her arm around Keys' waist, she pulls him against her.

"I know they have their duty, Barry. I just want Nick to come home to his parents and to us. They have some kind of name for the men who go down with their ships."

Keys turns them away from the waterfront to start walking back to the car. "They say those sailors are on eternal patrol. Nick knows the risks. He and his captain are experienced submariners. All we can do is say our prayers for them."

Early Monday morning Keys grabs the phone by the bed before the ringing wakes Mary.

"Yeah, whatta you want?" Keys cups his hand over the mouthpiece grumbling into the receiver.

"Get your ass in the office, Keys," Gray growls. "If you want to keep your job Washington wants you to clear your beef with Gamma."

Before Gray gets another word in, Keys growls back. "I don't want to keep it, Gray. You can have it." He hangs up the phone, then closes the receiver in the drawer of the nightstand before heading to the bathroom.

Chapter 35

After breakfast Keys and Mary discuss their finances. Keys has saved a good deal of money from his wages and so has Mary. Neither one of them did much spending while apart. Food, clothing, rent were the main items. Keys did spend $380.00 on his Kodak camera but expensed it on his taxes.

Marinships does not have a pension plan but Keys' years of service in the FBI will pay their food and rent with some left over. Mary takes down the numbers while they try to decide how much they can spend on an office and equipment to open the detective business.

The door bell rings, followed by knocking on the door. Keys gets up to answer. Jerry Walsh stands poised to knock again when Keys opens the door.

"You did it, you really did it?"

Keys laughs, standing aside to let Walsh in. "I really, really did it."

Walsh comes into the living room as Mary comes from the kitchen.

"Hi, Mary," Walsh says. "So you finally talked him into it, huh?"

"I didn't talk him into anything, Jerry. He had made up his mind before I came back." She strikes a pose with her hand behind her head. "I'm going to be the secretary."

"Well, I'll be darned. Congratulations all around." Walsh shakes Keys' hand and Mary gives Walsh a hug. Walsh hands Keys a small package. "This package came for you today at the office. I tried to call but your phone's been off the hook all morning. I was a little worried when you didn't come in. Gray's madder than a wet hen. He's been stormin' around the office barkin' like a dog all morning."

Keys puts the package on a table. "He'll get over it. Let's go get some lunch at Blum's. I'm feelin' expansive."

"Sounds good to me," Walsh says. "That brings to mind a great story I've got to tell Mary."

Keys playfully puts his hand over Walsh's mouth. "If it's what I'm thinkin' I'll break your neck."

"No, not Agent X10. I'll tell Mary that one when you're away on a big job."

After lunch Walsh returns to the FBI office. Keys and Mary go back to their apartment.

"You didn't open the package Jerry brought," Mary says.

Keys pulls off the paper covering a small box. Mary stands by his shoulder looking on. In the box is a silver dolphin's badge. Under the badge is a folded note. Keys hands the badge to Mary to unfold the note.

"It's from Nick." Keys holds the note so they can both read it.

Nick writes: " Barry, this badge always brought me luck and you need it more than I do. Your capacity to attract dangerous elements is second only to your affection for confection. I do have the badge I wear on my uniform so don't worry about me. I'll look for you both on the bridge if the Captain will let me. I look forward to your letters. Take Care, Nick."

"He is such a nice man, Barry. Keep that badge with you. I believe it will bring you luck."

Keys puts his arm around Mary to kiss her cheek. "I'll keep it in my pocket. Let's test it out. We'll go see what we can find for an office. I'd like to stay close to here. We can't afford the Hunter-Dulin but I wouldn't want be that close to old haunts anyway."

Coming out of the door onto Mason, big rain drops rain splatter on the sidewalk. Keys turns to Mary. "Well, maybe we should wait for another day."

Mary nudges Keys. "Look across the street, Barry."

On the front window of the building across the street a woman is placing a sign. Printed on the sign is Office for Rent Inquire Inside. Keys takes the Dolphin badge out of his pocket. Rubbing it with his thumb he says, "Maybe this really works. Shall we inquire inside?"

"We shall," Mary answers.

The office is small; the landlady adds two desks with chairs and a file cabinet to secure their signature on a lease. She calls a sign painter she knows to paint Keys Detective Agency on the window facing Mason Street.

"That badge works. I see fame and fortune in our future," Mary says.

Keys smiles, looking at Mary's bright face. "We've got a lot to do to get the office set up. Remember we have to be up early tomorrow to see Nick's boat go under the bridge."

The morning brings a light mist; fog rolls over the tops of the Golden Gate's towers. Mary and Keys wait on the North end of the bridge to get a better view of the bay. Mary pours hot coffee from a thermos while they wait. More people come onto the bridge to see their loved ones off.

Keys scans the bay with his binoculars; the mist makes it hard to see very deep into the bay. The morning's wet chill creeps through their coats. Keys sees a small destroyer escort coming toward them. Some distance behind is the *Bullshark*. "Here she comes." He hands the binoculars to Mary.

From the east, low in the sky the sun breaks through the mist. Mary tugs at Keys' coat. "There he is, Barry! He's with the officers on the bridge." She hands the binoculars to Keys to wave with both hands above her head.

Keys brings the binoculars to his eyes to see Nick on the bridge waving. He waves back as the *Bullshark* goes under them. They watch as the boat follows the destroyer out to sea. A rainbow forms an arch that the *Bullshark* passes under on her way to her destiny.

Mary takes the binoculars back from Keys. "My God, Barry, that is beautiful. I really hope that rainbow will bring them good luck. Nick will come back, I know he will."

###

Footnote 1

The Coe Letter

This letter was written by Lt. Cmdr Coe when he was CO of the *USS Skipjack*.

USS SKIPJACK
June 11, 1942
From: Commanding Officer
To: Supply Officer, Navy Yard, Mare Island, California
Via: Commander Submarines, Southwest Pacific
Subject: Toilet Paper
Reference: (a) USS HOLLAND (5148) USS SKIPJACK req. 70-42 of 30 July 1941.
(b) SO NYMI Canceled Invoice No. 272836
Enclosure: (1) Copy of Cancelled Invoice
(2) Sample of material requested.
1. This vessel submitted a requisition for 150 rolls of toilet paper on July 30, 1941, to USS HOLLAND. The material was ordered by HOLLAND from the Supply Officer, Navy Yard, Mare Island, for delivery to USS SKIPJACK.
2. The Supply Officer, Navy Yard, Mare Island, on November 26, 1941, cancelled Mare Island Invoice No. 272836 with the stamped notation "Cancelled---cannot identify." This cancelled invoice was received by SKIPJACK on June 10, 1942.
3. During the 11-3/4 months elapsing from the time of ordering the toilet paper and the present date, the SKIPJACK personnel, despite their best efforts to await delivery of subject material, have been unable to wait on numerous occasions, and the situation is now quite acute, especially during depth charge attack by the "backstabbers."

4. Enclosure (2) is a sample of the desired material provided for the information of the Supply Officer, Navy Yard, Mare Island. The Commanding Officer, USS SKIPJACK cannot help but wonder what is being used in Mare Island in place of this unidentifiable material, one well known to this command.

5. SKIPJACK personnel during this period have become accustomed to use of "ersatz," i.e., the vast amount of incoming non-essential paper work, and in so doing felt that the wish of the Bureau of Ships for the "reduction of paper work" is being complied with, thus effectively "killing two birds with one stone".

6. It is believed by this command that the stamped notation "cannot identify" was possibly an error, and that this is simply a case of shortage of strategic war material, the SKIPJACK probably being low on the priority list.

7. In order to cooperate in our war effort at a small local sacrifice, the SKIPJACK desires no further action be taken until the end of the current war, which has a created a situation aptly described as "war is hell."
J.W.Coe

The letter was given to the Yeoman, telling him to type it up. Once typed and upon reflection, the Yeoman went looking for help in the form of the XO. The XO shared it with the OD and they proceeded to the CO's cabin and asked if he really wanted it sent. His reply, "I wrote it, didn't I?"

As a side note, twelve days later, on June 22, 1942, J.W. Coe was awarded the Navy Cross for his actions on the S-39.

The "toilet paper" letter reached Mare Island Supply Depot. A member of that office remembers that all officers in the Supply Department "had to stand at attention for three days because of that letter." By then, the letter had been copied and was spreading throughout the fleet and even to the President's son who was aboard the *USS Wasp*.

As the boat came in from her next patrol, Jim and crew saw toilet paper streamers blowing from the lights along the pier and pyramids of toilet paper stacked seven feet high on the dock. Two men were carrying a long dowel with toilet paper rolls on it with the yards of paper streaming behind them as a band played coming up after the roll holders. Band members wore toilet paper neckties in place of their Navy neckerchiefs. The wind-section had toilet paper pushed up inside their instruments and when they blew, white streamers unfurled from trumpets and horns.

As was the custom for returning boats to be greeted at the pier with cases of fresh fruit/veggies and ice cream, the *Skipjack* was first greeted thereafter with her own distinctive tribute---cartons and cartons of toilet paper.

This letter became famous in submarine history books and found its way to the movie, *Operation Petticoat*, and eventually coming to rest (copy) at the Navy Supply School at Pensacola, Florida. There, it still hangs on the wall under a banner that reads, "Don't let this happen to you!" Even John Roosevelt insured his father got a copy of the letter.

The original is at Bowfin Museum in Hawaii.

Coming Up Next

Barry Keys will be back in *Agent Keys Steps Out*. His first big case as a private investigator will be back on Mare Island after black marketers.

Jack Novac will also be back in *Novac Strikes Back*. He goes back to Europe in 1944 planning to form an espionage ring with racers he met before the war on the continent.

Acknowledgements

Thanks to my wife Kathy for taking time from her busy schedule to produce the excellent cover art and to edit the text.

I want to thank all the volunteers working at the museum on Mare Island for their help. Joyce found a 1944 map of the shipyard for me to copy that I had searched for, for over a year. The ten-foot long map now adorns a wall of my writing office. Mare Island is a fascinating place to visit. Very helpful, knowledgeable folks.

Thank you to the Vallejo Naval and Historical Museum. I enjoyed the working submarine periscope.

Thank you to Janice Torbet of the San Francisco Main Library for her invaluable research. To all of the library staff there also, thank you. Everyone I came in contact with at main branch was extremely helpful.

Thank you to Kas and Peggy Kastner. They made some good suggestions with their edit. Kas, as only he can, told me great stories of his 1940's experiences. You'll read them in *Agent Keys Steps Out*.

Thank you to Kathy's great friend, Phyllis Gurney, for her suggestions.

For those of you who would like see what the inside of the *Bullshark* was like, you can take an excellent virtual tour of the *SS Pampanito* from your computer. It is the same Balao class boat as the fictional *Bullshark*. The link is www.maritime.org/pamphome.htm.

About the Author

I started racing for Group 44, the factory Triumph sports car team on the East Coast. After winning a national championship, I moved to California to race the new Titan Formula Ford for the West Coast distributor.

I raced for forty years, competing in TransAm, IMSA, Formula Atlantic, and FIA endurance races. I drove factory cars for Triumph, Porsche, Datsun, and Titan. I won the last championship with a sports car I designed and built at my company, Downs Engineering. Downs Engineering builds race cars, specialty cars, and Hayabusa racing engines. Please visit our website, http://www.downsengineering.com.

I live in Northern California with my lovely wife, Kathy.

The website where you bought your book should have a review option. Reviews are really helpful to me. I'm interested in learning what you enjoy reading so I can continue to make my books fun for you to read. And reviews are the way the book distributors rank the books in their sales lists so other readers can find them.

Reviewing can be as easy as clicking stars, or as detailed as you would like to make your comments.

In any case, I really appreciate your interest in my work.

Connect with me on online

Mike Downs Mysteries website;

http://www.mikedownsmysteries.com.

Facebook: Mike Downs

Twitter: #Mike Downs Author

Goodreads: Mike Downs